Mary Cumberland Alcock

Poems, &c. &c.

Mary Cumberland Alcock

Poems, &c. &c.

ISBN/EAN: 9783337157944

Printed in Europe, USA, Canada, Australia, Japan

Cover: Foto ©Andreas Hilbeck / pixelio.de

More available books at **www.hansebooks.com**

P O E M S,

&c. &c.

BY THE LATE

Mrs. MARY ALCOCK.

LONDON:

PRINTED FOR C. DILLY, POULTRY.

M.DCC.XCIX.

TO THE READER.

THIS Volume, which the Editor now refpect-
fully prefents to her kind Subfcribers in particular, and to the Public in general, contains very
nearly the whole of what fhe could collect from
amongft the papers of her deceafed Aunt, in any
degree fit for publication, and more perhaps than
by choice fhe would have publifhed, was fhe not
perfuaded that this fmall Collection will fall into
the hands of few readers, but fuch as have patro-
nized and promoted her undertaking through regard to the memory of the amiable Author. All,
to whom the virtues of her character were known,
will be candidly difpofed to excufe any trivial er-
rors in her compofition. She never held herfelf up
as a writer: when fhe reforted to her pen, it was
either to amufe a leifure hour, to gratify an abfent
friend, or for the fublimer purpofe of pouring out
her heart in praifes and thankfgivings to her God.
The Editor thinks herfelf fortunate in having been

able

able to collect fome, from amongft many Poems of this defcription, which, fhe has reafon to believe, her Aunt had written and neglected to preferve : they were the fecret afpirations of her unobtrufive piety, and as fuch, fhe kept them private ; for in her blamelefs compofition vanity had no part. Once only fhe reforted to the prefs ; but in that fingle inftance fhe concealed her name, and, from motives of pure benevolence only, publifhed her *Fragment* for the relief of the debtors in Ilchefter gaol ; her charitable motives were fully gratified by the refult, for many debtors were liberated out of their confinement at Ilchefter, and fourteen out of Newgate, by the produce of that little Poem.

During her refidence at Bath, fhe occafionally fubfcribed her tribute to the *Vafe* at Bath-Eafton, and fome few of thefe will be found in the following Collection. The little Effays in profe are trifles, which fhe never had in idea to communicate, except to a female relation, with whom fhe corre-

fponded,

fponded, and for mere amufement interchanged fome papers in the fame ftile, but which were foon difcontinued : it is in pure obedience to the wifhes of fome particular friends that they are now inferted.

It may be matter of information to fome readers to premife, that Mrs. MARY ALCOCK was the daughter of Dr. DENISON CUMBERLAND, bifhop of Kilmore, in Ireland, by JOANNA, daughter of the learned Dr. RICHARD BENTLEY. Born of fuch parents, and defcended in a line from fuch anceftors (for her father was grandfon to that great and good man, bifhop CUMBERLAND, of Peterborough) this excellent woman feemed to have concentrated in her heart the full fpirit of their piety and benevolence. It may without exaggeration be faid, that the fimple journal of her time on earth would be a record of good deeds, moft honourable to her memory, and a leffon to the world at large. The afflictions, which it pleafed Providence to vifit her

with,

with, were of a very peculiar nature, such as a spirit so gentle, and feelings so refined as her's, seemed ill able to contend with; but though nature had assigned her a corporeal frame so extremely feeble and defenceless, that every blast of the elements might be supposed to threaten it with extinction, Heaven had endowed her with a soul equal to the severest trials, and capable of the sublimest efforts. In her piety she found resources against every species of worldly misfortune, and under circumstances, which none but minds like her's could have surmounted, she stood forth as the benefactress and protectress of a whole orphan family of dependant Nieces, of which the humble Editor of these slight memorials of her genius is one, not indeed the most fortunate, but surely not the least forward to confess her favours, to bewail her loss and to revere her memory.

JOANNA HUGHES.

Mrs. MARY ALCOCK died on the 28th day of May 1798, in the 57th year of her age. Exhausted by long illness, which she endured with undiminished patience, she expired, without pain or struggle, in the house of her beloved friends and affectionate relations, Mr. and Mrs. ASHBY, of Haselbeach, in Northamptonshire, and was buried in the parish church of that village. The following inscription, upon a plain marble tablet, is about to be erected to her memory in that Church.

———

" This Tablet is set up by the surviving friends of
" Mrs. MARY ALCOCK,
" to signify that within this Church,
" beneath the pavement of the middle aisle,
" her perishable remains are buried.

" At the resurrection of the Just,
" When the Spirits of the Blessed shall ascend into glory,
" We believe and are persuaded,
" That the soul of this inestimable woman,
" Whose whole life was exercised in every Christian duty,
" Whose faith was firm,
" Whose piety was sincere,
" And whose benevolence was universal,
" Shall be found worthy, thro' the trials of this mortal life,
" And the merits of her ever blessed Redeemer,
" To be received into the mansions of eternal happiness."

SUBSCRIBERS.

His Royal Highnefs GEORGE PRINCE of WALES.
Her Royal Highnefs the PRINCESS of WALES.
Her Royal Highnefs PRINCESS SOPHIA.
Her Royal Highnefs PRINCESS AMELIA.

A

ANCASTER, Duchefs of
Albemarle, Countefs Dowager of
Ailefbury, Countefs Dowager of
Apreece, Lady
A'Court, Lady
Afhby, George, Efq. 6 Copies
Afhby, Mrs. 6 Copies
Afhby, Rev. George
Apreece, S. A. Efq.
Apreece, Mrs.
Apreece, Mifs
Ainflie, Mrs.
Andre, Mifs
Andre, Mifs A.
Ackworth, B. B. Efq.
Allix, John, Efq.
Allix, Mrs.
Allix, Mrs. Charles
Arden, Mrs.

Afkew,

Afkew, Mifs
Andrew, Rev. Robert
Allen, Captain, Royal Navy
Akers, Mrs. 2 Copies
Anderfon, John, Efq.
Abbott, Mrs.
Acland, Mrs.

B

Bath, Marchionefs of
Buckinghamfhire, Earl of
Buckinghamfhire, Countefs of
Bentinck, Lord Edward, 6 Copies
Bentinck, Lady Edward, 6 Copies
Bagot, Lord
Bellingham, Lady
Barrington, Honourable Mrs.
Barnard, General
Barnard, Mrs.
Benyon, Mrs.
Batley, Mrs.
Budge, William, Efq.
Bowdler, Thomas, Efq.
Bowdler, Mifs
Bowdler, Mrs. H.   3 Copies
Badcock, William, Efq.
Badcock, Mrs.
Bannifter, Mifs
Bannifter, John, Efq.
Bulkley, Col. Coldftream Regiment
Burnett, John F. Efq.
Burnett, Mrs.
Brereton, Mrs.

Brent,

Brent, Timothy, Efq.
Bolton, William, Efq.
Bentley, Mrs. James Cumberland
Brickwood, Mrs.   2 Copies
Bird, Henry Merttins, Efq.
Bird, Mrs. Merttins
Bland, Jofeph, Efq.
Bagot, Honourable, Efq.
Baker, Captain
Bainbridge, Launcelot, Efq.
Benfon, Rev. Martin
Bowes, Mifs,   3 Copies
Benfield, Mrs.
Book Society, Ladies
Burney, Rev. Charles, LL. D.
Burney, Mrs.
Barrett, Mrs.
Bryan, Mifs
Bernard, Mrs.
Bludworth, Mrs.
Blifard, Mrs.
Benfon, Mrs.
Breafe, Mr.
Bacon, Mrs.
Buckle, Mifs
Bainbridge, Mifs Mary
Bertie, Mrs.
Buckner, Mifs
Beaver, Rev. James, *Corp. Chrift. College, Oxford*
Bullivant, ———, Efq.
Bullivant, Mifs
Bateman, Mifs
Bunny, Mrs.

                                        Booth,

Booth, Mrs. Ann, 2 Copies
Butt, Mrs.
Burdett, Mifs
Burdett, Mifs Frances
Bofcawen, George, Efq.
Blencowe, Colonel
Blencowe, Mrs. 2 Copies
Barwell, Mrs.
Baldwin, Mr. John
Baldwin, Mrs.
Baldwin, Mifs
Bullock, John, Efq.
Bingham, Mrs.
Braithwaite, ———, Efq.
Barker, Mifs
Boddington, Samuel, Efq.

C

Clarendon, Earl of
Compton, Hon. Lady Frances
Caftleftewart, Lady
Clonbrook, Lady
Cumberland, Lady Albinia
Cave, Rev. Sir Charles
Cave, Lady
Cave, Mifs
Collins, John, Efq.
Collins, Mrs.
Collins, Mifs
Cowper, William, Efq.
Carter, Mrs. Elizabeth
Cumberland, Richard, Efq.
Cumberland, Mrs.

Cumberland,

Cumberland, Mifs
Cumberland, Captain Charles
Cumberland, Captain William, Royal Navy
Clark, Mrs.
Crefwell, Mifs
Calvert, Mrs. T.
Coote, Mrs.
Cotten, ————, Efq.
Cotten, Mrs.
Cotten, Mrs. S.
Coxe, Mrs.
Cox, Mifs
Cox, Mifs C.
Carden, James, Efq.
Courthope, Mrs.
Carlyle, Rev. Doctor
Carlyle, Mrs.
Cornforth, Mrs.
Cartwright, Edmond, Efq.
Chriftie, Mifs
Clarke, Mrs.
Coxe, Mrs. E.
Chriftie, Mrs.
Corbett, Robert, Efq.
Corbett, Mrs.   2 Copies
Caldwell, Mifs
Curtance, Mifs
Cotten, Rev. Mr.
Campbell, Mifs
Cocks, Mifs.   2 Sets
Cookfon, Mrs.
Clayton, Mrs.
Cornwallis, James, Efq.
Creffe, Mrs.

Childers,

Childers, Mrs.
Cooper, Mrs.
Cipriani, ———, Esq.
Chapeau, Mrs.

D

Durham, Bishop of
Dundas, Lady Jane
Dormer, Sir Clement Cotterel
Dormer, Lady Clement Cotterel
Dashwood, Mrs.
Dashwood, Mrs. A.
Dashwood, Miss
Dalton, Mrs.
Durham, Captain, Royal Navy
Downes, Rev. Andrew, 2 Copies
Downes, Mrs. 2 Copies
Day, Thomas, Esq.
Davis, Mrs. J.
Dumbleton, Mrs.
Dobbs, ———, Esq.
Dixon, Mr. Richard
Douglas, Mrs.
Denison, Mrs.
Denton, Miss
Dickenson, C. Esq.
Du Cane, Mrs. Mary
Du Cane, Miss
Donavon, Mrs.
Dougan, Mrs.
Dod, Miss Mary Ann
Doughty, Robert, Esq.
Doughty, Mrs.

Davis,

Davis, P. Esq.
Dawson, Mrs.

E

Englefield, Sir Henry, Bart.
Englefield, Lady
Edwards, Lady
England, Major General
Etherington, Colonel
Etherington, Major
Ellis, John, Esq.
Ellis, Mrs.
Evans, Mr. } 11 Copies
Evans, Mrs.
Ekins, Mrs. S.

F

Fielding, Lady
Frodderly, Lady Edward
Foote, G. T. Hatley, Esq. 2 Copies
Foote, George, Esq. jun.
Foote, Rev. Robert
Foote, Mrs. Robert
Foote, Mrs. John
Foote, Mrs.
Foote, Miss
Fanshaw, Mrs.
Fanshaw, Miss
Fraser, Mrs.
Fryer, Henry, Esq.
Francis, Rev. J. E.
Fourdrinier, Mrs.
Frankland, Mrs.

Fauntleroy,

Fauntleroy, Mrs.
Farquhar, Mrs.
Fremeaux, Mifs E.
Forbes, Mrs.
Forth, Mrs.   2 Copies

G

Gloucefter, Bifhop of
Graham, Sir James, Bart.
Graham, Lady Catharine
Graham, Rev. Mr.
Graham, Mrs.
Glynn, Doctor
Green, Thomas, Efq.   3 Copies
Green, Mrs.   3 Copies
Green, John Cheale, Efq.
Green, Mrs.
Green, Mrs.
Green, Mrs.
Green, Rev. Thomas
Gordon, Mrs. George
Gulftone, Frederick, Efq.
Gulftone, Mrs.
Gayfere, Mits
Gwathie, Mrs.
Greaves, Mrs.
Gray, Charles Gordon, Efq.
Gray, Mrs.   2 Copies
Gould, Mrs.
Gofling, Mrs.
Garratt, Mrs.   3 Copies
Ginger, Mr.
Ginger, Mrs.

Ginger,

Ginger, Mr. William
Girardot, Andrew, Efq.
Girardot, Mrs.
Gale, Mrs.
Gower, Mifs
Gilpin, Mrs.
Gordan, Mrs.
Grenville, General
Gitfon, Mr.
Gibbes, Mrs. 2 Copies
Gibfon, John, Efq.
Greame, Charles, Efq.

H.

Harborough, Earl of
Harborough, Countefs of
Hartley, Lady Louifa
Hawley, Sir Henry, Bart.
Hawley, Lady
Hefketh, Lady
Herries, Lady, 2 Copies
Hanbury, William, Efq.
Hanbury, Mrs.
Hanbury, Mifs
Hartopp, Sir Edmond
Hatfell, John, Efq.
Hatfell, Mrs.
Hervey, Doctor
Hervey, Mrs. Elizabeth
Hunter, Mrs.
Halhed, Mrs.
Henderfon, Francis, Efq.
Henderfon, Mrs.

Hurd,

Hurd, Captain, (Royal Navy)
Hurd, Mrs.
Holroyd, Mrs.
Hunt, Mifs
Horft, Mrs.
Heydon, Mrs.
Hobfon, George, Efq.
Hay, Captain, (Royal Navy)
Hurft, Mr.
Hughes, Rev. William
Hughes, John, Efq.   6 Copies
Hughes, Mifs E.
Hornage, Mrs.
Hiflop, Mrs.
Harman, Mr.   2 Copies
Hungerford, Mrs.
Harrifon, Mrs. Frances
Hervey, Mr.
Hind, Mr. Charles
Hart, Mrs.

I.

Ifham, Lady
Jones, Lady
Ifham, Mrs.
Jones, Mifs
Jackfon, Francis, Efq.
Jackfon, Mrs.
Jackfon, Mifs
Ifted, Mrs.   3 Copies
Ifted, Mifs
Ifted, Mifs R.
Ifted, Mifs C.

Jephfon,

Jephfon, Major
Jephfon, Mrs.
Ifted, Samuel, Efq.
Ifted, Mrs. S.
Johnfon, Mifs
Jefferies, Mifs
Jekyle, Mifs
Iremonger, Mifs

K.

King, Admiral Sir Richard
King, Mifs
Knatchbull, Charles, Efq.
Knatchbull, Mrs. Charles
Knatchbull, Mrs. Joe
Kerr, Mrs.   3 Copies
Kenfington, Mrs.
Kenfington, Mifs Charlotte
Kingfcote, Thomas, Efq.
Kingfcote, Mrs.
Knight, Mrs.
Knox, David, Efq.
Kinderfly, Mrs.
Kemble, John, Efq.
Kemble, Mathew, Efq.
Kemble, W. Efq.

L.

London, Bifhop of
Leeds, Duke of
Leeds, Duchefs of,   3 Copies
Litchfield, Bifhop of

Lumley,

Lumley, Lady Sophia
Lilford, Lord
Lilford, Lady
Langham, Dowager Lady
Langham, Sir William
Langham, Lady
Langham, Mifs
Langham, Mifs C.
Langham, Mr.
Lofack, Richard Hawkfhaw, Efq.
Lofack, Mrs.
Lofack, Richard, Efq.
Lofack, Mrs. Richard
Lofack, Colonel
Lofack, Captain, (Royal Navy)
Lofack, Lieutenant Woodley, (Royal Navy)
Lloyd, Mrs.
Lafcelles, William, Efq.
Lambert, William, Efq.
Lambert, Daniel, Efq.
Langton, ——, Efq.
Ledge, Mrs.   3 Copies
Long, William, Efq.   6 Copies
Long, Mrs.   3 Copies
Leech, Mr.   3 Copies
Lofh, Mr. James
A Lady.
Legge, Honorable Captain, (Royal Navy)
Lill, Mrs.
Latham, Mrs.   2 Copies
Latham, Mifs
Latham, William Afhby, Efq.
Latham, Mrs. Afhby

Lamb,

Lamb, Mrs.
Lucas, Mrs.
Lindon, —— Efq.

M.

Mount Edgecomb, Earl of
Mount Edgecomb, Countefs of
Monfon, Lady Dowager
Monfon, Lady
McDenald, Lady Louifa
Montgomery, Lady Mary
Merrick, Lady Lucy
Mildmay, Lady
Mann, Sir Horace
Mann, James, Efq.
Mann, Mrs.
Mann, Mifs
Montagu, Mrs.
Murray, General
Murray, Mrs.
Manning, William, Efq. M. P.
Manning, Mrs.
Merrick, Mrs.
Money, General
Maude, Mrs.
Mac Doughty, Mrs.
Morley, Rev. Thomas Wilfon, } 6 Copies
Morley, Mrs.
Marfhall, Mr.
Myers, William, Efq.
Merle, Mrs.
Moore, James, Efq.

Munn,

Munn, Mr. 2 Copies
Martin, James, Efq. M. P.
Martin, Mrs.
Marfh, Commiffioner
More, Mrs. Hannah
Mathews, Lieutenant, 89th Regiment
Morris, Mrs.
Melmoth, Mrs.
Maynard, Thomas, Efq.
Maynard, Mrs.
Metcalfe, Mrs.
Maltby, Mifs
Mathews, Mrs. B.
McKenzie, Captain, 23d Regiment
Madden, Lieutenant Colonel, Staffordfhire Militia
Mowbray, Captain, Royal Navy
Moore, Captain, - ditto
Mayhew, Chriftopher, Efq.
Maunfel, Mrs.
Maddock, John, Efq.
Maddock, Mrs.
Maddock, Mafter Afhby
Marfhall, Mrs.
Myddelton, Rev. Doctor, 3 Sets
Myddelton, Mrs. Robert
Myddelton, Rev. John
Middelton, Mrs.

N.

Northampton, Countefs of
Northefk, Lord
Northefk, Lady
Neale, Sir Harry Burrard

Neale,

Neale, Lady H. Burrard
Neville, Chriftopher, Efq.
Neville, Mrs.
Noel, Lieutenant Colonel
Nicholls, the Rev. Robert Bouchier, Dean of
  Middleham, 3 Copies
Norton, George, Efq. 3 Copies
Newbolt, Rev. Mr.
Nicolay, Frederic, Efq.

O.

Orlebar, Richard, Efq.
Ord, Mrs.
Ottley, A. Efq.
Orlebar, Mrs. 2 Copies
Otway, Mrs.
Oglevie, Mifs
O'Brien, Captain, (Royal Navy)

P.

Peachy, Lady
Peyton, Lady
Parker, Admiral Sir Peter
Parker, Mifs
Porteus, Mrs.
Pownall, Lieutenant Colonel } 3 Sets
Pownall, Mrs.
Pownall, Mrs.
Pownall, Mifs
Pownall, J. Lillingfton, Efq.
Pownall, Mrs. J. L.
Pownall, Mrs.
Pery, Mrs. J.

Pratt,

Pratt, Mrs.

Peele, Rev. Mr.

Peele, Mrs.

Preſt, Mrs.

Patrick, Mrs.

Perceval, Honorable Mrs.   3 Copies

Pitt, Thomas, Eſq.

Pitt, Mrs.

Parſons, William, Eſq.

Pelham, Mrs. Creſſet Pelham

Powys, Mrs.

Phillips, Captain, 44th Regiment

Partley, Mrs. T.

Pares, Thomas, Eſq.

Pares, Miſs,   2 Copies

Pares, Mrs.

Pares, Thomas, Eſq. jun.

Pares, John, Eſq.

Pares, Rev. William

Pares, Mrs.

Powis, Rev. Littleton

Payne, John, Eſq.

Payne, Rene, Eſq.

Popple, John, Eſq.

Pennant, David, Eſq.

Pennant, Mrs.

Phillipps, Thomas March, Eſq.

Phillipps, Mrs.

Phillpps, Miſs

Padley, Mrs.

Packe, Charles James, Eſq.

Packe, Mrs.

Packe,

Packe, Miſs
Packe, Miſs Frances
Packe, Miſs M.

R.

Robinſon, Sir George, 6 Copies
Robinſon, Lady, 3 Copies
Robinſon, Mrs.
Reynolds, Richard, Eſq. } 20 Copies
Reynolds, Mrs.
Reynolds, Mrs.
Robertſon, Colonel, (Weſtminſter Volunteers)
Robertſon, Mrs.
Rambouillet, Mrs.
Randolph, Mrs.
Rie, Mrs.
Relfe, Mr.
Relfe, Mr. J.
Ray, Mrs.
Reade, Mrs.
Reade, Miſs
Reade, John, Eſq.
Reade, Mrs. John
Rocke, Mrs.
Roſe, Mr. (Surgeon, Coldſtream Regiment)
Rogers, Samuel, Eſq. (Author of the Pleaſures of
        Memory)
Ridge, Thomas, Eſq.
Ridge, Mrs.
Ridge, Mr. Thomas
Raſhleigh, Mrs.
Romney, George, Eſq.   3 Sets
Ricketts, Mrs.

Ricketts,

Ricketts, Mrs. George
Ridſdale, Mrs.
Rolleſon, Major
Rills, Mrs.
Reade, Edward, Eſq.
Rogers, S. Eſq.
Rogers, Henry, Eſq.
Rokeby, Mrs.
Rokeby, Miſs
Richards, Miſs
Roberts, Miſs Eleanora
Rawlinſon, ——— Eſq.
Ruddſhall, Richard, Eſq.

S.

Sheffield, Lady
Shipley, Mrs.
Shipley, Miſs
Strode, Mrs.
Sotheby, Mrs.
Shaw, John, Eſq.
Satterthwaite, Mrs.
Staunton, Mrs.
Sturges, Rev. Mr.
Stranbenzee, Mrs.
Sharp, Miſs
Sharp, Richard, Eſq.
Sykes, Sir Francis
Sykes, Lady
Savage, Mrs.
Savage, Benjamin, Eſq.
Savage, Mrs. B.
Smith, Mrs.

Smith,

Smith, Miſs
Smith, Mr.
Story, Rev. Philip
Story, Mrs.
Story, Miſs
Spencer, Henry, Eſq.
Stuart, Charles, Eſq.
Stanley, Mrs.
Somarfall, Thomas, Eſq.
Somarfall, Miſs
Somarfall, Miſs Mary
Smith, Mrs.
Smith, Mrs.
Smith, Mrs.
Strutt, Mrs.
Sheriff, Mrs. 2 Copies
Stewart, Mrs. Charles
Straitfield, Mrs. 3 Copies
Short, Mrs.
Stower, Captain, 24th Regiment
Salkeld, Thomas, Eſq.
Shaw, Rev. Mr.
Southbey, Miſs
Seward, William, Eſq.
Sharp, William, Eſq.
Sharp, Miſs
Squire, Mr. William
Stockdale, Rev. William
Stephenſon, Mrs.

T.

Talbot, Rev. William
Talbot, Mrs.
Thomas, Rev. J. B. D.

Terry,

Terry, Mrs.
Taylor, Miſs Mary
Thomas, Thomas, Eſq. 2 Copies
Thomas, Mr.
Thomas, Miſs
Thompſon, Mrs. 3 Copies
Thompſon, Peter, Eſq.
Townley, Miſs
Towne, Rev. Mr.
Towne, Mrs.
Trower, H. Eſq.
Trower, Mrs.
Tippet, Mrs.
Taylor, Rev. Mr.
Tatham, Mrs. 2 Copies
Tuſton, J. F. Eſq.
Thornton, Rev. Robert
Train, Mrs.
Thornton, Mrs. jun.
Tymns, Mrs. George
Thompſon, Narbonne, Eſq.

V.

Villars, Lady Charlotte
Vaughan, Mrs. 2 Copies
Vaughan, Mrs.
Vanſittart, Mrs.
Vaux, Mrs.
Vanneck, Honourable Mrs.
Vanburgh, Mrs.

Warwick,

W.

Warwick, Earl of, 6 Copies
Warwick, Countefs of, 6 Copies
Wilfon, Lady
Wilfon, Rev. George
Wilfon, Mrs.
Wright, Henry, Efq. 3 Copies
Wright, Mrs.
Wraight, William, Efq.
White, Doctor, Royal Navy
White, Mrs.
Walter, John, Efq.
Walter, Mifs
Walter, William, Efq.
Walter, John, Efq. jun.
Williams, Mrs.
Woodington, Mifs
Wathen, Mr.
Winftanley, Mrs.
Webfter, Mrs.
Waughs, Mrs. 3 Copies
Walters, Mrs. 5 Copies
Wilkie, Mrs.
Wingfield, Rev. Charles
Whalley, Mrs.
Wigglefworth, Mrs.
Whitaker, Mrs.
Weftern, Mrs. Frances
Weftern, Rev. Sherley
Weftern, Rev. Walfingham
Weftern, Mrs.
Watfon, Mifs

Walter, Mrs.
Willes, Rev. Mr.
White, Mr.
Whalley, Rev. Palmer
Whalley, Mrs. S.
War, Mifs S.
Wilsford, Mrs.
Williams, Gregory, Efq.
Williams, Mrs.

Y.

Young, Dowager Lady,   3 Copies
Young, Mr.
Young, Mrs.
Young, Profeffor
Young, Mrs.
Young, Mrs.
Young, Mrs. Robert
Young, Mifs
Young, Doctor
York, Mrs.

CONTENTS.

Hymn

CONTENTS.

P O E M S.

✦c✦✦c✦

A VISION.

METHOUGHT a boundlefs plain entranc'd I view'd,
Beyond what waking eye could ever fcan,
With thoufand and ten thoufand flocks beftrew'd,
Emblems, I foon defcried, of fallen man.

Thro' tangled wilds and crooked ways with fpeed
Numbers I faw on numbers heedlefs run,
Yet oft they ftopt to crop each pois'nous weed,
That fhew'd it's gaudy colours to the fun.

B   With

With grief I mark'd their fleeces torn and rent,
As thro' the brambles eagerly they rufh'd,
Some, on their own and other's ruin bent,
Turn'd round enrag'd, and at each other pufh'd.

The young their folds and fertile vales forfook,
And vent'rous climb'd the wild and craggy rock,
But foon the wolf the ftraggling lamb o'ertook,
Who rafhly dar'd to leave the parent flock.

A general bleating now affail'd mine ear
In tones expreffive of the deepeft woe;
" Alas!" I cried, " are there no fhepherds near,
" No guides the ftrait, the even way to fhow ?"

When turning to the Eaft my enquiring eye,
(With double ftrength it's vifual pow'r renew'd)
The main, the beaten path I did efpy
Th; ' verdant vales with guides and folds beftrew'd.

" Ah,

" Ah, wretched sheep," lamenting then I cried,
" Why leave ye thus your folds and fost'ring guides?
" Undone ye are, and, lost by your own pride,
" Ye shun those helps which bounteous Heav'n provides."

But oh! how can my feeble verse pourtray
The glorious vision, which I then survey'd,
When all resplendent as the blaze of day,
The Shepherd came in majesty array'd?

Such heav'nly light refulgent beam'd around,
Swift o'er the wide expanse I saw it spread,
Such words benignant in mine ears did sound,
As cheer'd the living and reviv'd the dead.

Methought all nature seem'd to bloom anew,
The barren desert blossom'd as the rose,
The parched wilderness appear'd to view
As pastures green, where living water flows.

There

There at his foothing call, and fafe from harm,

With tendereft care his flocks the Shepherd fed,

The feeble lambs he gather'd with his arm,

And gently thofe that were with young he led.

Obedient to the heavenly Shepherd's call,

Gafping with thirft I hafted to the ftream,

There in his prefence on my knees I fall,

Then wake, and ftart from my enraptur'd dream.

WRITTEN ON NEW YEAR'S DAY.

———

Doth not, my foul, each circling year
Remind me that I muft appear
   Before my heav'nly King,
In whofe bleft fight man's longeft age
Is but a momentary ftage,
   That flits on fwifteft wing?

Then fay, thou pure, thou heav'n-born fire,
Why doft thou not with fond defire
   Subdue this inward fear?
So might I with afpiring mind
Prefs on, nor caft a look behind,
   Nor figh to linger here.

My will moſt freely I reſign
To thee, my judge, oh! make it thine
  In word, in deed, in thought:
So ſhall I find contentment here,
Nor ſhrink from death, tho' death draw near
  With all his terrors fraught.

No ſting in death but ſin is found,
And ſince our God hath heal'd that wound,
  What have we here to dread?
'Tis our's to praiſe Him and obey,
Look up to Him from day to-day,
  To give us heav'nly bread.

Teach me to wait with humble truſt,
To hope the beſt, nor fear the worſt
  In this life's varying round;
And when I meet misfortune's blow,
Teach me ſubmiſſion, that may ſhow
  On what my joys I found.

Oh

Oh then vouchfafe thy heavenly aid
To lead me thro' the gloomy fhade
   Of worldly grief and care;
Supported by thy foft'ring hand,
Let me temptation's lure withftand,
   And chace away defpair.

Thus fhall you pafs ferenely o'er,
Ye circling years, whilft I implore
   The God, who gives me breath,
To lead me on from day to day
Secure in virtue's holy way,
   Refign'd to life or death,

THE ROSE TREE AND THE POPPY.

A FABLE.

DEEP in a lone fequefter'd grove
   A beauteous Rofe-tree grew;
It's bloffoms breath'd perfume as frefh
   As morn's ambrofial dew.

Each fpreading branch luxuriant ftrew'd
   The verdant turf below,
And high it's blooming head it rear'd,
   And made a lovely fhew.

Yet not it's flowers of choiceft hue,
   It's branches fpreading wide,
It's lofty head or rich perfume
   Provok'd one fpark of pride.

Humbly

Humbly to every breeze it bow'd,
    That gently fann'd each tree,
And courteously difpens'd it's fweets
    To the induftrious bee.

Near to it's moffy ftem there fprung
    A flower fpontaneous-bred,
A fingle Poppy, 'twas no more,
    It's hue a vivid red.

With envy fir'd, the Poppy cried—
    Your boughs exclude the light,
Your fmell affects my head, in fhort,
    You're odious to my fight.

Your fhatter'd leaves beftrew the ground,
    Your dew-drops fall like tears,
Your ftraggling buds grow wild and rude,
    Your thorns alarm my fears.

What

What tho' you deck Belinda's breaſt,
  Or twine in Delia's hair,
You never long enjoy your bliſs,
  But droop and wither there.

What tho' the painter may compare
  Your tints with Chloe's bloom,
Or poet madly may exclaim,
  Her breath is your perfume.

Such flattering rhapſodies may plant
  Sharp thorns in Chloe's breaſt,
Like thoſe that arm thy venom'd ſtalk,
  And rob her mind of reſt.

Whilſt I am known of ſovereign power
  To calm the aching ſenſe,
So ſoporific is my juice,
  Such peace can I diſpenſe.

'Tis I can lull the monarch's care,
 I blunt the edge of pain ;
Then fay, thou fplendid trifling fhrub,
 If I am born in vain.

But thou with indolence fupine,
 In garden or in grove,
Art only form'd to be the food
 Of poetry and love.

But that I longer fcorn to plead,
 Or half your faults relate,
Elfe could I tell how oft you've caus'd
 Commotions in the ftate ;

Commotions of the deepeft dye,
 With your own kindred bred ;
Witnefs the well known feuds betwixt
 The White-rofe and the Red.

Such

Such rebel livery I difdain,
    Tho' white as pureft fnow ;
You're only in falfe colouring dreft
    To ftrike the deadlier blow.

The Poppy paus'd—when thus the Rofe
    In accent mild replied :
Ah ! let us not in conteft try
    What we can ne'er decide.

Know that 'tis Providence beftows
    To each it's proper fhare ;
Thus you receive a healing power,
    Whilft I may be more fair.

Then let us each our lot receive,
    And thankfully improve,
So fhall your enmity be turn'd
    To friendfhip, peace, and love.

Ah, had not envy touch'd your root,
   In me no faults you'd found;
But ftoop your head, and deign to view
   Thofe Daifies on the ground.

No gaudy colouring can they boaft,
   No healing power have they;
Yet ftill they fmiling fill their fpace,
   And thus they feem to fay:

" Learn mortals, learn to be content,
   " Let pride and envy ceafe,
" So fhall your ways be ftrew'd with flowers,
   " And all your paths be peace."

WRITTEN ON EASTER DAY.

GLAD tidings hath my Saviour brought
  To cheer the drooping mind,
And mighty wonders hath he wrought
  This day for loft mankind.

Awake ! caft off the works of night,
  The facred page explore,
There view how life is brought to light,
  And there thy God adore.

There thou may'ft drown each flavifh fear,
  There hear thy God proclaim
Peace and falvation far and near
  To all, who love his name.

Can

Can gratitude, can duty move ?
    Can faith or hope infpire ?
Doth pious zeal, doth fervent love
    Thy foul with ardour fire ?

Here may thy mind with full delight
    Each faculty employ ;
Here, rapt in thought, bring to thy fight
    Immortal fcenes of joy.

For as our dear Redeemer rofe,
    And overcame the grave,
We may in his bleft word repofe,
    And He our fouls will fave.

Death is no longer now our foe,
    Nor can for victory ftrive ;
For fince by man came death and woe,
    By Chrift we're made alive.

                            Methinks

Methinks I look beyond this scene
 Of pain, and grief, and fear,
To manfions where our God shall reign,
 And wipe away each tear.

What heart but muft with rapture burn
 To meet fuch heav'nly love !
Come then, my foul, and ftrive to earn
 The joys that are above.

Be ftedfaft then, thy faith maintain,
 In goodnefs ftill abound ;
So fhall thy labour not be vain,
 But by thy God be crown'd.

ON SENSIBILITY.

―――――

I F e'er to Friendſhip's call you lent an ear,
Or ſympathyſing dropt the ſoothing tear,
Oh, Senſibility, receive my prayer !
Attend, and pardon that I ſeek to know,
If in a world ſo fraught with various woe,
Thy votaries find thee moſt their friend or foe.
Thy joys and griefs alike let me ſurvey,
Then fairly aſk thee if thy joys repay
Thoſe pangs, which ſoon or late the heart will rend,
Where thou art nouriſh'd as the gentleſt friend,
When rude misfortune, with reſiſtleſs ſway,
Tears from that heart what moſt it loves away;
Whilſt feelingly alive to every pain,
Thro' thee it taſtes each ſorrow o'er again;

Thus,

Thus, crufh'd beneath Affliction's heavieft blow,
It bears a double weight of human woe:
Ah cruel, thus to fteal into the heart,
And cherifh'd there to act a traitor's part.

Come then, Indifference, thou eafy gueft,
Aflume the empire o'er my tortur'd breaft,
And by thy trifling, pleafing, giddy fway,
Chace every heart-corroding pang away;
Teach me another's griefs unmov'd to hear,
And guard my eye againft the falling tear;
Drive recollection from her inmoft feat,
Nor let my heart with agitation beat;
Be thou my champion thro' life's varying round,
And fhield my bofom from the flighteft wound.

Yet paufe awhile! and let me take a view,
Left with the pains I lofe life's pleafures too.
Say, doth not duty, love, and friendfhip give,
The greateft pleafures we can here receive;

And

And can a heart untouch'd by others woe,
The joys of friendſhip, love, and duty know ?

    If ſuch the purchaſe to be freed from pain,
Oh, Senſibility, to thee again
I turn—do thou my every thought control,
'Tis thine to animate or ſoothe the ſoul ;
'Tis thine alone thoſe feelings to beſtow,
From which the ſource of every good doth flow;
Since theſe thy joys, thy griefs I'll patient bear,
And humbly take of each th' allotted ſhare ;
To Friendſhip's ſhrine the ready tribute bring,
And fly to Sorrow on Compaſſion's wing,
Enjoy the good, againſt the worſt provide,
By taking Reſignation for my guide,
In her ſafe conduct patiently ſubmit
To every pain, which Providence thinks fit.

A HYMN.

My God, whofe all-pervading eye
Scans earth beneath and heav'n above,
Witnefs if here or there thou fee'ft
An object of mine equal love.

Not the gay fcenes, where mortal men
Purfue their blifs, and find their woe,
Detain my rifing heart, which fprings
The nobleft joys of Heav'n to know.

Not all the faireft fons of light,
That lead the army round thy throne,
Can bound it's courfe, it preffeth on,
And feeks it's reft in God alone.

Fixt

Fixt near the immortal ſource of bliſs,
Firm and undaunted it ſurveys
Each ſhape of horror and diſtreſs,
That Earth combin'd with Hell can raiſe.

This feeble fleſh ſhall faint and die,
This heart renew it's pulſe no more;
Ev'n now it views the moment nigh,
When life's laſt movements ſhall be o'er.

Thou vanquiſh'd King of Terrors, come!
With thine own hand thy power deſtroy;
Approach, and bear my ſoul to God,
My portion and eternal joy.

THE CHIMNEY-SWEEPER'S COMPLAINT.

A CHIMNEY fweeper's boy am I;
   Pity my wretched fate!
Ah, turn your eyes; 'twould draw a tear,
   Knew you my helplefs ftate.

Far from my home, no parents I
   Am ever doom'd to fee;
My mafter, fhould I fue to him,
   He'd flog the fkin from me.

Ah, deareft Madam, deareft Sir,
   Have pity on my youth;
Tho' black, and cover'd o'er with rags,
   I tell you nought but truth.

My

My feeble limbs, benumb'd with cold,
   Totter beneath the fack,
Which ere the morning dawn appears
   Is loaded on my back.

My legs you fee are burnt and bruis'd,
   My feet are gall'd by ftones,
My flefh for lack of food is gone,
   I'm little elfe but bones.

Yet ftill my mafter makes me work,
   Nor fpares me day or night;
His 'prentice boy he fays I am,
   And he will have his right.

" Up to the higheft top," he cries,
   " There call out chimney-fweep!"
With panting heart and weeping eyes
   Trembling I upwards creep.

But

But ſtop ! no more—I ſee him come ;
 Kind Sir, remember me !
Oh, could I hide me under ground,
 How thankful ſhould I be !

THE HIVE OF BEES:

A FABLE, WRITTEN IN DECEMBER 1792.

In antient legends of paſt time we find,

Birds, beaſts, and inſects us'd to ſpeak their mind,

And oft by fable ſerious truths impart

To mend the morals and to ſtrike the heart :

Nay Solomon himſelf would deign to ſay,

Go to the Ant, thou ſluggard! learn her way.

But now alas! in theſe degenerate times,

Inſects have learn'd from men to ape their crimes,

The fable's turn'd—falſe morals now are ſhewn

In place of true—a ſad reverſe you'll own.

A hive of bees within a certain grove

Had long enjoy'd contentment, peace, and love,

Fed

Fed on each fource of fweet that earth beftows,

Ev'n from the cowflip to the ftately rofe;

Each morn had fipp'd of dew from Heav'n, which fell

And lodg'd in filver'd cup or golden bell;

Had drawn the nectar of each fragrant flower

To carry treafures to their native bower,

And there in cells of curious form they ftor'd

Their feveral tributes to the general hoard;

Then fafe at night were fhelter'd by thofe bowers,

Where firft they fwarm'd, when in their infant hours:

Each morn they fallied with the rifing fun,

Nor e'er returned until their tafk was done;

For arts and induftry had made them great,

And feemingly had fix'd their happy ftate;

A ftate, where nature's policy doth trace

To every bee his ftation, rank, and place:

Some form'd to labour for the public good,

Others to nurfe the young, and chew their food;

Some on the watch as centinels between

Whatever danger may affail their queen;

For

For every hive is in itfelf protected,
Whilft to it's fovereign it is well affected.

But now no further to dilate my ftory,
This hive, when at it's higheft pitch of glory,
Like other ftates did fubjects ftill contain
Of difcontented mind and heated brain,
Prone to adopt and lead fome new opinion,
Spurning reftraint, and grafping at dominion;
Thefe oft with greedy lift'ning ear repair'd
Clofe to a neighb'ring hive, from whence they heard
A murmuring hum, as if from difcontent,
Of liberty, no queen, no government;
Let all be equal, and thefe lordly drones
Be fet to work to fhape thefe ugly cones :
'Tis flavery I fwear—no more will I
Lag home with honey in my bag and thigh,
Much fooner will I dart my fting and die.

Thus faying, oft their meafures they'd debate,
And in convention plot againft the ftate;

But here diforder mark'd their wretched way,
Each claim'd his right, a right to bear the fway,
And left the loyal bees their haunts fhould fee,
They dar'd not light upon a flower or tree,
Where aught of fubftance, fit for daily food,
Might be extracted for the public good;
But confcious of their bafe intent, they fhun
Whatever fpreads its bloffoms to the fun,
And to the deadly nightfhade darkling flew,
Or on the hemlock fwarm'd, or pois'nous yew,
And there their mifchiefs hatch'd in fell debate,
There plann'd the downfal of their queen and ftate :
So loud they buzz'd their murmurs thro' the trees,
Of liberty, no work—the rights of bees—
That echo fwift convey'd the infectious found,
And Liberty—no work—rebellow'd round.

Their plot now ripe, they act the fatal fcene,
Murder the guards, and then confine their queen :

Rebellion

Rebellion buzzes thro' the ftraw-built dome—

" Seize, feize the honey, and lay wafte the comb!

" Deftroy each cell, for labour now is o'er,

" We'll feaft and revel on the public ftore."

And now how gladly would I draw a veil

O'er the remaining fequel of my tale;

But recent facts require I fhould relate

How bad example marr'd the happy ftate.

Tho' moft with horror heard the foul difgrace

Brought on the nobleft of the infect race,

Yet thofe who had enlifted in the plan,

And long'd like them to copy after man,

Now vend their poifons, and in treafons dire

Againft their friends, their queen, their hive confpire,

Whilft fwarms from forth the rebel ftate combine

To profecute the horrible defign,

And, fhame to tell, tho' courteoufly receiv'd,

League againft thofe by whom they are reliev'd.

Arous'd

Arous'd at length, the loyal bees unite
To fave their ftate, and arm them for the fight,
True to their fovereign, who with gentle fway
So mildly rul'd, 'twas freedom to obey;
And now behold them eager and alert
To expel the traitors and their fchemes avert;
Taught by examples terrible as thefe,
That faction blafts the happinefs of bees,
Active they keep their vigilance alive
To guard their monarch, property, and hive.

ON THE HUMAN HEART.

SAY, for you know, ye fecret fprings
   Which guide the human heart,
Whence comes it that fuch trivial things
   Give mine fo keen a fmart?

Mine, which hath known fuch real woes,
   Such real ills hath borne;
If having ftood fuch weighty blows,
   Why by a touch o'erthrown?

Thus have I feen the fturdy oak,
   Which hardly deigns to bow
When the ftorm rages, by the ftroke
   Of the fharp axe laid low.

The bark, which winds and waves had brav'd
   On many a hoſtile coaſt,
At length from foreign dangers ſav'd,
   In it's own port is loſt.

If from a friend a word I hear,
   Or meet a look unkind,
Why from mine eye deſcends the tear,
   And why this tortur'd mind?

And why will thoſe we love thus give
   Theſe ſmall, tho' deadly, ſtings?
How ſain would I no grief receive
   But what from Nature ſprings!

Thoſe ſorrows may I learn to bear,
   And humbly kiſs the rod,
Thro' faith and hope caſt off deſpair,
   And give my ſoul to God.

ON PLEASURE.

———

PLEASURE, hail, thou welcome theme,
Chief purfuit of mortal race,
Pleafing phantom, fairy dream,
Lead me to thy dwelling place.

There in feftive mirth and joy
Smoothly glide the fportive hours;
There no cares, no griefs annoy,
Where thou ftrew'ft thy golden fhowers.

Long thy fuppliant fought in vain
To defcry this blifsful feat,
Oft I've view'd thy fmiling train
Beckon to thy foft retreat.

D   But

But when near the mountain top,
Where thine airy caftle ftands,
Down the beauteous pile would drop.
Mould'ring into barren fands.

Quick the funfhine difappears,
Sudden ftorms and tempefts roar,
Sorrow leads her train in tears,
Wrecks beftrew th' affrighted fhore.

Take, oh take me from the fight,
Left my heart with grief fhould break;
In yon vale I fpy a light,
Let me to that cottage make.

Oft I've read, in humble life
Pleafure with Content doth dwell,
Grandeur leads to pain and ftrife,
Joy reigns in the lowly cell.

There

There in Virtue's lap reclin'd,
Let me feek at leaft for reft,
Tis not in this world defign'd
Man fhould be completely bleft.

Happieft when he fcorns to woo
Pleafures, which, at length obtain'd,
Reafon's calmer joys fubdue,
Quick t' efcape, tho' flowly gain'd.

Teach me then, thou power benign,
Who can'ft lafting blifs difpenfe,
How to reach thofe joys divine,
Bleft reward of innocence.

Teach me in my prefent ftate
Cheerfully to bear each ill,
With fubmiffion calmly wait
Th' appointment of thy heav'nly will.

Then

Then when tranfient pleafures ceafe,
And pain and grief alike are o'er,
Receive me to thefe realms of peace,
Where Pleafure dwells for ever more.

ON WHAT THE WORLD WILL SAY.

═══

Of all the foolish vain pretences,

That mortals use to cheat their senses,

   This has the greatest sway—

Not that, which conscience dictates right,

Tho' clearly mark'd as day from night,

   But what the World will say.

To this, as to some idol god,

Who rules us with an iron rod,

   We sacrifice each day;

Our time, our judgment, and our ease

Alike bow down this shrine to please

   Thro' fear what it might say.

Thus

Thus fubject to it's bafe control,

We check each motion of the foul,

 Which points to Reafon's way,

Left, varying from the giddy throng,

We rudely fhew them they are wrong,

 What would they then not fay?

While motives weak as thefe prevail,

We turn with every fhifting fail

 Of Fafhion's pow'rful fway,

Down her impetuous tide we're hurl'd,

Loft to each comfort in the world,

 Thro' fear what it might fay.

Thus like fome heedlefs bark we're toft,

Till foundering on that very coaft

 Where all our treafure lay,

Deferted and forlorn we lie,

Unpitied by each ftander-by,

 Nor cheer'd by what they fay.

        Oh

Oh could the World that peace beſtow,

Which, courting it, we all forego,

    Our toils it well would pay;

But ſince the ſad reverſe we find,

'Tis nought but madneſs e'er to mind

    What ſuch a World can ſay.

THE BODY-POLITIC.

If in the Body-politic you fee
Rebellion, rapine, bloodfhed, anarchy,
That ftate you fay is loft ! So when you find
The body human with diftemper'd mind,
The blood corrupted, and the fever high,
You doubt not to pronounce—that man muft die.

Now in the way of Fable we'll fuppofe
Rebellion in the human frame arofe ;
Each member loudly founded forth his merit,
And cried, t' obey the Head fhew'd want of fpirit ;
'Twas time the Limbs fhould now affert their part,
And overturn the empire of the Heart.

The ſtubborn Knees declar'd no more they'd bend
For God or King, nor any ſtrength would lend
To bear a Head of ſuch unwieldy ſize;
To hear and ſee requir'd not Ears and Eyes;
All parts were equal, and had each a right
T' aſſume the gift of hearing and of ſight.

Whereat the Feet ſtept forth with furious ſound
Stamping and ſwearing they'd not touch the ground;
Henceforth aloft they'd riſe erect in air,
And make the daintier Hands the burden bear.

This ſaid, the Hands indignant caught th' alarm,
And ſtruggling tried to ſeparate from the Arm;
Aloud they clapp'd, and ſummon'd all to fight
To fix their freedom, and enforce their right.
And now Convulſion ſeiz'd on every part,
Loud beat each Pulſe, and terror ſhook the Heart;
Within was heard a horrid noiſe and rout,
The *Inſide* claim'd the right to be the *Out*.

The

The Lungs protefted they'd not draw the breath ;
They car'd not if it brought on inftant death ;
'Twere better all were loft than they denied
The right to hold a fhare in the Outfide.

The Stomach roar'd he foon wou'd ftop digeftion,
If e'er his outfide right was call'd in queftion :
The Veins declar'd they'd not perform their part,
Nor longer throw the blood up to the Heart;
The Heart might feed itfelf, or yield it's place
To thofe, who'd fill it with a better grace.

On this the Liver writh'd himfelf around,
And fwore that long, though rotten and unfound,
He'd fought that place ; he now would feize the throne,
For he was fit to rule, and he alone.
This rous'd the Spleen, who on the vitals fed,
Planning by craft the downfal of the Head ;
But now o'ercharg'd with envy, rage, and guile,
In hafte he rofe, and overfet the Bile.

The

Thus all within was agony and ſtrife,

Each freſh convulſion feem'd to threaten life;

The Limbs diſtorted riſe—they give the blow,

And foon the Head (fo honour'd once) lay low.

And now behold the Body's wretched ſtate,

Taught by this ſad example, ere too late,

That ſuch each Body-politic muſt be,

Where foul rebellion reigns and anarchy.

WRITTEN AT HARROWGATE.

———

LET all, who would efteem it good
   To fight 'gainft death and fate,
Ufe no delay, but hafte away
   To drink at Harrowgate.

At this bleft well, tho' ftrange to tell,
   However weak your ftate,
You may enfure a perfect cure,
   Such pow'r has Harrowgate.

Should gout or rheum your life confume,
   Or palfy fhake your pate,
Whate'er your ill, drink but your fill,
   You're well at Harrowgate.

If madnefs dire, with brain on fire,
  Each nerve fhould agitate,
Deep in this fpring, plunge headlong in,
  You're heal'd at Harrowgate.

From forth thefe ftreams proceed fuch fteams
  Each fenfe to ftimulate,
That in one feafon your perfect reafon
  Returns at Harrowgate.

Then hither fpeed, for moft have need
  Their brains to reinftate,
Ah ne'er look back, you're on the rack
  Till fafe at Harrowgate.

Should anxious care, or dull defpair,
  Or envy's deadly hate,
Torment your mind, you'll quickly find
  Them fly from Harrowgate.

Kind

Kind friends, good fare, and pureft air,
    Your wits fo animate,
That here in verfe you may rehearfe
    The charms of Harrowgate.

Then let me úfe my proffer'd mufe,
    Nor think I arrogate
Too high a praife, to fwell my lays
    In hailing Harrowgate.

There may be feen, at Thackwray's Queen,
    In peaceful happy ftate,
Hufband and wife, devoid of ftrife,
    Such power hath Harrowgate.

Each beau and belle, at this pure well,
    Their fpirits recreate,
That here you'll find them much inclin'd
    To mirth at Harrowgate.

No

No party rage doth here engage
　　Their hours in fell debate;
Good reaſon why—ill humours fly
　　Away from Harrowgate.

On pleaſure's wing, they ſweetly ſing
　　The joys that on them wait,
They play, they laugh, they dance and quaff
　　Their glaſs at Harrowgate.

From morn till eve, you may believe,
　　Their time they diſſipate;
The reaſon why—they cannot die,
　　They're ſafe at Harrowgate.

Then hither ſpeed, you all have need,
　　'Tis death to heſitate;
Make no delay, but poſt away,
　　And meet at Harrowgate.

INSTRUCTIONS,
SUPPOSED TO BE WRITTEN IN PARIS,
FOR THE MOB IN ENGLAND.

===

O f Liberty, Reform, and Rights I fing,

Freedom I mean, without or Church or King;

Freedom to feize and keep whate'er I can,

And boldly claim my right—The Rights of Man:

Such is the bleffed liberty in vogue,

The envied liberty to be a rogue;

The right to pay no taxes, tithes, or dues;

The liberty to do whate'er I chufe;

The right to take by violence and ftrife

My neighbour's goods, and, if I pleafe, his life;

The liberty to raife a mob or riot,

For fpoil and plunder ne'er were got by quiet;

The right to level and reform the great;

The liberty to overturn the ftate;

The

The right to break through all the nation's laws,

And boldly dare to take rebellion's caufe :

Let all be equal, every man my brother ;

Why one have property, and not another ?

Why fuffer titles to give awe and fear ?

There fhall not long remain-one Britifh peer ;

Nor fhall the criminal appalled ftand

Before the mighty judges of the land ;

Nor judge, nor jury fhall there longer be,

Nor any jail, but every pris'ner free ;

All law abolifh'd, and with fword in hand

We'll feize the property of all the land.

Then hail to Liberty, Reform, and Riot !

Adieu Contentment, Safety, Peace, and Quiet !

PSALM CXXXIX.

O Lord my God! to thee is known
My rifing up, my fitting down;
My path, my bed thou art about,
And all my ways thou fpieft out.

For lo! thou underftandeft, Lord,
My every thought, my every word;
Oh, ever guide my tongue, my heart,
For thou haft fafhioned every part.

Such knowledge how fhould I attain?
Such wond'rous goodnefs how explain?
Say, would I from thy prefence flee,
Ah, whither?—I am ftill with thee.

If to the Heav'n of Heavens I climb,
Thou'rt there in majefty fublime;
Or if to Hell I downwards go,
Behold, O Lord, thou'rt there alfo.

If on the morning's wing I foar,
Or dive where deepeft oceans roar,
Ev'n there thy prefence fhields from harm,
And guides me with thy mighty arm.

If in the dark and midnight hour
I feek to hide me from thy power,
That darknefs is to Thee as bright
As orient beams of morning light.

When in my mother's womb I lay,
Thou fafhionedft my wond'rous clay,
Nor were my bones before my birth
Unfeen, tho' form'd beneath the earth.

Thine

Thine eyes my fubftance did defcry,
When hid from ev'ry mortal eye,
And in thy book each member plac'd,
As day by day their forms were trac'd.

Thy councils, Lord, to me how dear!
The fum how great beyond compare!
As well might I the fands recount,
As tell them o'er, fo great th' amount.

Wilt thou not, Lord, the wicked flay?
Depart, ye finful men, away!
For lo! thine enemies, O Lord,
Deny thy name, and flight thy word.

Do not I hold them in defpite,
Who rife againft thy caufe to fight?
Yea, more I hate their impious ftrife,
Than if they warr'd againft my life.

Try

Try me, O God, my heart refine,
Reprove it, make it wholly thine;
Look well if unreveal'd there lie
One fin remote from human eye.

A HYMN.

—

Omniscient source of love divine!
 Who reign'st supreme above,
Deign to accept with look benign
 This little pledge of love.

To thee, my Saviour and my King,
 What debts of praise I owe;
Oh teach my soul those strains to sing,
 The virtuous only know.

'Twas Thou, that bad'st my feeble frame
 From mould'ring dust to rise;
Thy spirit breath'd the vital flame,
 O Lord, supremely wise.

Thy gracious care preferv'd my youth,
  Of life the tendereft ftage,
Oh may thy providence and truth
  Protect my riper age.

If when the furious ftorms attack,
  My haplefs thoughts fhould ftray,
Direct, O Lord, the wanderers back
  Thine own almighty way.

The firft affaults of fin defeat,
  Deftroy the tempter's power,
Secure my foul from all deceit,
  And guard it every hour.

So fhall my rapturous heart with joy
  Thy heavenly name adore,
Thy praife my grateful tongue employ,
  Till time fhall be no more.

AN AUNT'S LAMENTATION FOR THE ABSENCE
OF HER NIECE.

WRITTEN FROM HASTINGS.

———

Like as the dove I fit alone,
   Dejected, pale, and wan,
Without a friend to hear me moan
   The lofs of Marianne.

Now on the raging deep I gaze,
   And all it's wonders fcan,
Yet ftill my thoughts revert always
   To thee, my Marianne.

Now o'er my book, my work I pore,
   But do whate'er I can,
My book, my work will charm no more,
   I've loft my Marianne.

The

The other morn the fifers play'd,
 I to the window ran,
And as the mufic pafs'd, I faid,
 Where, where is Marianne?

Oft as I hear the failors bawl
 For Sufan or for Nan,
Alas, I cry, Oh that a call
 Would bring me Marianne!

Now on the beach forlorn I ftray,
 Nor know the face of man,
Yet all would pleafe, each fcene be gay,
 Had I my Marianne.

With her each hour I could employ,
 And ftill new pleafures plan,
For ev'ry hour 'twould be my joy
 To pleafe my Marianne.

Ah

Ah could I view her face I'd fly
From Beerfheba to Dan,
No land, no fea beneath the fky
Should part my Marianne.

ON THE

DEATH OF DAVID GARRICK, Esq.

―――

How oft haſt thou, great maſter of thine art,

Call'd forth each feeling from the human heart,

With admiration fill'd the wondering mind,

And made exiſt what Shakſpeare's pen deſign'd,

With valour fir'd, with horror chill'd the breaſt,

Now footh'd with love, and now with grief oppreſt,

With frantic madneſs rent th' aſtoniſh'd ear,

Or from the eye made flow the pitying tear;

Then, as the merry Muſes led the way,

And bade thee all thy comic powers diſplay,

How didſt thou charm and captivate each ſenſe,

The champion both of wit and eloquence.

No more alas ! thine accents charm the ear,

No feigned forrows now draw forth the tear,

Deep is the grief, fincere the tears we fhed,

Garrick, alas ! lies number'd with the dead.

THE CONFINED DEBTOR.

A FRAGMENT FROM A PRISON.

" Sick and in prison,
And ye visited me."

This Poem hath been published, and the profits arising from the sale were appropriated towards the release of the debtors confined in the county gaol at Ilchester for small sums. The benevolent intentions of the author were fully rewarded by the success of the sale, and a list of the debtors discharged in consequence thereof was published in the daily papers.

Note by the Editor.

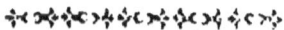

The following Lines are offered to the Public, not as a Poem, but as a true, though faint, description of the miseries of a prison!— Should they have the effect wished for of calling forth the attention of the charitable towards the release, or relief, of a number of most wretched debtors now confined in Ilchester gaol, the donations for them will be received and acknowledged in the papers by Mr. Gye and the Proprietors of the Circulating Libraries.

Advertisement by the Author.

THE CONFINED DEBTOR.

From thefe drear cells, where cheerlefs horror reigns,
Midft the dread found of groans and clank of chains,
Where life is death, and day perpetual night,
Say ! Shall a wretch like me prefume to write ?
A wretch cut off from ev'ry focial tie,
Expell'd from life, yet not allow'd to die,
At once, from wife, from children torn away
By thofe, who make calamity their prey ;
Who dart with more than tygers' favage rage
On pining ficknefs, or decrepid age :
Can fuch a wretch with trembling hand affay
His manfion and companions to portray,
And griefs proclaim which ne'er have met the day ?
Griefs, which no tongue can fpeak, or pencil paint,
Which mock all forrow, and make language faint,

Bring

Bring scenes to light as Erebus profound,
Where murderers dire lie shackled to the ground,
And innocence and guilt alike are bound!
Yet could I to my sad companions gain
One ray of hope, 'twould mitigate my pain!

Oh were my lines in Heaven's own language drest,
Then would they pierce and rend each human breast,
Expand each heart, and make each eye o'erflow,
At these dread scenes of wretchedness and woe.

Yet tho' no poet's fire inspires my pen,
I write to *Christians* and I write to *Men*,
I write to those (if Heav'n direct it so)
Whose hearts dilate at every human woe,
To those whose charity with healing hand
Diffuses health and blessings o'er the land,
Who condescend to search the hidden cells,
Where pining want in silent anguish dwells.

There

There, in obedience to their Lord divine,
They bind the wound, and pour in oil and wine !

What joys they feel, who follow fuch a guide !
Joys ! which exceed all human worldly pride,
Joys ! which e'en death itfelf cannot deftroy,
For then they " enter on their Mafter's joy !"
Oh did the proud and felfifh but believe
How far more bleft to *give*, than to *receive !*
Did but the flaves of pomp and grandeur know
What ftreams of comfort from their wealth might flow !
Waters ! as pure as morning dews, which rife
From lofty mountains till they reach the fkies,
Defcending thence, as tender drops of rain,
They cheer each valley, and each thirfty plain ;
So when in gratitude the widow's pray'r,
The pris'ner's fighs reliev'd, the orphan's tear
To Heav'n afcend, an offering pure and neat,
A bleft memorial and an odour fweet,

F   Recorded

Recorded ſtands, from thence they ten-fold pour
Their precious ointment, as the grateful ſhow'r !

Ah me ! what means that ſhriek, that horrid yell,
Thoſe bitter oaths, which ſink the ſoul to hell ?
Say, loſt companions, in this dread abode
Do ye ne'er think of an offended God ?
Ne'er ſeek by pray'r, by penitence and ſighs,
T' obtain that pardon, which the world denies ?
Ah ! ſue for mercy with your lateſt breath,
And trembling aſk for pardon after death.

* * * * * * * * * * * * * * *
* * * * * * * * * * * * *

* * * * * * * * * * * * * *

* * * * * * * * * * * * * *

No, No, I'll curfe not e'en that fatal morn,

Which faw me to this loathfome prifon borne;

Snatch'd from my homely bed, where long I'd lain

Struggling with ficknefs, poverty and pain,

Yet ftill kind hope, (the wretch's lateft friend)

Did frequent comfort with my forrows blend;

For near my couch the partner of my care

Would anxious watch, and bid me not defpair,

Whilft fhe with life and ftrength, by Heav'n fupply'd,

Could yield that help, ficknefs to me deny'd,

Could by her diftaff earn that homely bread,

By which our helplefs children long were fed:

She bade me hope by induftry fet free,

No griping landlord need we dread to fee,

She taught me to fupprefs the rifing figh,

And check'd the tear when ftarting from mine eye;

She

She o'er my limbs her thread-worn garment ſpread,

And with her infants clothes ſuſtain'd my head,

Whilſt at my feet thoſe infants playful ſmil'd,

And by their prattle oft my pains beguil'd !—

Ah ! helpleſs babes, ah ! wretched, deareſt wife !

More lov'd by me than liberty, or life,

No more thy ſoothing voice now charms mine ear,

And gently whiſpers that no danger's near,

No more my playful infants cheer my ſight,

Here all is horror and perpetual night !

Hope can no longer now ſuppreſs my ſighs,

Or check the tears when ſtreaming from mine eyes.

Still, ſtill I feel that pang, which rent my heart,

Still do I hear thy ſcreams when forc'd apart,

Still view thy pallid face, all bath'd in tears,

My children's cries ſtill vibrate in mine ears,

Still feel them cling around my trembling knees,

While on their helpleſs parent bailiffs ſeize,

Still, ſtill I hear my wife, my children call—

" Have patience, patience, and we'll pay thee all !"

Remorſeleſs

Remorfelefs creditor, thou'ft done the deed!

Nor tears, nor prayers, nor innocence could plead!

Oh! had thine heart one fpark of pity known,

To griefs like ours it had compaffion fhewn!

Come! fee thy captive! view his wretched ftate,

And fhew fome mercy ere it be too late;

Think! will this noifome air, and clay-cold floor,

His feeble frame to ftrength and health reftore?

Oh could he liberty and ftrength regain,

To pay thy debt he ev'ry nerve would ftrain!

Will grief and anguifh aid the wretched wife

In earning food to fave each infant's life?

Ah! rather will not frenzy and defpair

Deprive thofe infants of a mother's care?

Methinks e'en now, within this dungeon foul,

I hear her vent her agony of foul.

* * * * * * * * * * * * * * *

* * * * * * * * * * * * * *

* * * * * * * * * * * * * * *

F 3   Yet

Yet let not thoughts like thefe diftract my brain,

Thoughts, which heap woe on woe, and pain on pain;

No! rather let me, with imploring eye,

Look up to Him, who hears the pris'ner's figh;

To Him, who calls the weary and opprefs'd,

To come to Him for fuccour and for reft!

Who, tho' forlorn and helplefs here I lie,

Without one pitying friend or comfort nigh,

May caufe fome tender fympathizing heart

To foothe our forrows, and relief impart,

Some heart, replete with love, to whom 'tis giv'n

Thofe *bounties* to difpenfe, which flow *from Heaven!*

THE 55TH PSALM.

―――

Hear, oh my God ! thy grace extend,
Hide not thyfelf, O Lord, from me!
Hear my petition, and befriend
The mournful caufe I plead to thee !

The enemy with ceafelefs ftrife,
Their minds on mifchief ever fet,
Malicioufly purfue my life,
And impious men their caufe abet.

My heart's difquieted with dread,
The fears of death are on me come,
With ghaftly horrors overfpread
And tremblings, I expect my doom.

F 4

Then

Then did I wifh with filver wings
Dovelike to fly and feek my reft,
Far from the fource whence forrow fprings,
In fome lone wild to make my neft.

With hafte I would efcape and fly,
Or ere the ftorm takes hold of me :
Deftroy their tongues, for I efpy
How wickedly they ftrive with thee.

The city walls both night and day
With mifchief they encompafs round ,
Deceit and guile are in their way,
Sorrows within their ftreets abound.

Were it an enemy declar'd,
That wrought this fhame, an open foe,
From fuch difgrace I had been fpar'd,
And 'fcap'd the meditated blow.

'Twas

'Twas thou, my counfellor and guide,
Companion and familiar friend,
With whom I commun'd fide by fide,
As to God's houfe we did afcend.

Them death fhall haftily o'ertake,
And whelm them quick into the grave;
But as for me my pray'r I'll make
To God, whofe power alone can fave.

At evening and at early dawn,
At noon-day alfo will I pray,
So fhall He hear my voice, nor fcorn
To lead my foul in his right way.

The God, who all things doth behold,
Th' eternal King and Lord of all,
Will hear my pray'r, and me uphold,
So that I fhall not greatly fall.

'Tis

'Tis He, that from the battle's rage
My foul to fafety hath reftor'd,
He can their furious wrath affuage,
He is the only God and Lord.

ADDRESSED TO SLEEP.

Descend, sweet Sleep, mine eyelids close
   With peace-restoring balm;
'Tis thou alone can'st heal my woes,
   And lull me to a calm.

Come then on Fancy's airy wing
   With all thy pleasing train,
Thy kind delusions with thee bring,
   And lull my aching brain.

But why so oft must I in vain
   Invoke thy sov'reign power?
Say, cruel, why dost thou disdain
   On me thy bliss to shower?

Freely

Freely by Heav'n on all thou'rt fhed,
　　The gift all nature fhares,
Why then from me fo diftant fled ?
　　Ah ! why not hear my pray'r ?

Why, like the felfifh and the vain,
　　Thus deaf to forrow's cry,
Court none but Pleafure's fmiling train,
　　And fhun the weeping eye ?

Did wicked thoughts within my breaft
　　A welcome harbour meet,
Did I, when lying down to reft,
　　Plot or contrive deceit,

Then could I not prefume to find
　　Remiffion of my grief ;
For whither can a guilty mind
　　Refort for its relief ?

But

But foft ! fure 'twas a voice that faid—

   " Stop ! thy rebukes are vain ;

" Man by his Maker firft was made

   " Exempt from grief or pain."

WRITTEN IN IRELAND

———

How bleſt would be Iërne's iſle,
Were bigotry and all it's guile
   Chac'd as a cloud away ;
Then would Religion rear her head,
And ſweet Contentment round her ſpread,
   Like a new dawn of day.

Come then, oh come, thou Truth divine !
With double radiance deign to ſhine,
   Thy heavenly light expand ;
'Tis thine to chaſe theſe clouds of night,
Which darken and confound the ſight
   In this divided land.

Attendant

Attendant on thy profp'rous train
I fee fweet Peace with honeft gain
   Spread wide her liberal hand,
While Difcord, mafk'd in deep difguife,
Abafh'd from forth her prefence flies,
   Struck by her magic wand.

Around, where now in ruins lie
Thy facred altars, I efpy
   Fair Order rear each pile,
Whilft o'er thy wilds forlorn and wafte,
Lo, Induftry with nimble hafte
   Makes hill and valley fmile.

No more thy fons in fell defpite,
A murderous band *array'd in white,*
   Shall deal deftruction round;
Each man beneath his vine fhall reft,
No more by Bigotry oppreft,
   But Truth by Peace be crown'd.

                        Then

Then fhall Iërne tune her lyre,
And with united voice confpire
  To hail her happy ftate ;
All hail, Iërne, Nature's pride,
No more fhall wars thy land divide,
  Wert thou as good as great.

MODERN MANNERS.

———

Of modern Manners let me fing,
   The gay Flirtilla cries—
Manners, my dear ! there's no fuch thing—
   Her grandmamma replies.

You fay, cries Mifs, in days of yore
   People were highly bred ;
But, thank my ftars, thofe days are o'er,
   Thofe people all are dead.

The world is now at eafe and gay,
   Improv'd in every art,
Fraught with diverfions night and day
   To charm and fire the heart.

To live in thefe enlighten'd days
 Is furely life indeed ;
Long may they laft, Flirtilla prays,
 And joy to joy fucceed !

The mind, left free and uncontroul'd,
 Makes pleafure all it's aim ;
Youth will not now by age be told—
 My dear, you are to blame.

Such Gothic parents, thanks to Heaven,
 Are now but rarely found ;
Thofe, whom the fates to me have given,
 Live but in Pleafure's round.

No tedious hours at home they pafs
 In dull domeftic care ;
To think, they fay, would foon, alas !
 Bring wrinkles and grey hair.

Oft

Oft have I heard them jeer and joke
   At wedlock's galling chain;
Then cry, Thank Heaven, 'tis now no yoke,
   We wed to part again.

In former times indeed 'twas said,
   That hearts were join'd above,
That women to their hufbands paid
   Obedience, truth and love.

But title, pin-money and dower
   Now join our hands for life,
No other ties than thefe have power
   To couple man and wife.

To thefe alone my thoughts afpire,
   On thefe I fix my heart;
A wealthy hufband I require—
   I care not when we part.

ON RAILLERY.

WRITTEN IN MAY 1781, FOR THE VASE AT BATH-EASTON.

A SUBJECT fo copious, fo flow'ry and gay,
Suits well to the fportive amufements of May,
But fcorn'd be the mufe, unrewarded the rhime,
Tho' it fweetly fhould flow and in melody chime,
If ever in earneft my pen or my heart
In raillery's caufe fhould be found to take part;
If ever, the ftrength of this talent to fhow,
A friend I fhould teaze or embitter a foe;
If ever, when aiming my wit to difplay,
Be my verfe e'er brilliant, or meafure fo gay,
By raillery's tinge I difcolour its lay.
No, rather affift me, ye mufes benign,
Who prefide o'er this Urn and it's myrtles entwine,

To

To guard well it's laurels from every annoy,

That innocent humour might damp or deftroy;

Ah, fhield from it's lafh every bard, who effays

To folicit your favour and merit the bays;

May the brow of each youth with your laurels be
    crown'd,

Who can rally with wit, and yet ne'er give a wound;

May the breaft of each nymph your chafte myrtle
    adorn,

Who her lover ne'er rallied, or treated with fcorn;

May they ne'er know the pangs, that a poet fuftains, ⎫

Who morning and night having puzzled his brains, ⎬

Is raill'd at and laugh'd at and hifs'd for his pains. ⎭

Hail, genuine good humour, good breeding and fenfe,

This circle you guide and it's humour difpenfe;

Your favour I court, but if I fhould fail,

I fhan't be furpriz'd, but I never will rail.

THE

8TH, 9TH, AND 10TH VERSES

OF THE 57TH PSALM.

———

AWAKE, my glory, ere the rofy morn
Shall with a vivid blufh the fkies adorn,
Before the fun arife to break the day,
Awake, and chace thy gloomy fleep away.

Awake, foft lute, awake, my tuneful lyre,
With facred tranfports my warm breaft infpire;
Awake, each faculty, awake and fing
In holy rapture to my heav'nly King.

In

In notes divine let my glad verfe proclaim
His mighty goodnefs and eternal name;
Let my loud praifes thro' the world refound,
Whilft wond'ring nations liften all around.

But, O my God, thy wonders are too great
For tongue to fpeak, or verfe to celebrate,
So vaft thy mercies and thy truth fo high,
They pierce the clouds and reach beyond the fky.

HYMN.

May peace and love from God above
My bofom ever fill,
So fhall I find an humble mind
Obedient to his will.

May faith and truft, and all that's juft,
My foul with ardour fire,
I feek not wealth, I afk but health,
Nor more would I defire.

May thanks and praife, throughout my days,
My heart and mind employ,
So fhall I know, whilft here below,
More than an earthly joy.

A RECEIPT FOR WRITING A NOVEL.

Would you a fav'rite novel make,
Try hard your reader's heart to break,
For who is pleas'd, if not tormented ?
(Novels for that were firſt invented).
'Gainſt nature, reaſon, ſenſe, combine
To carry on your bold deſign,
And thoſe ingredients I ſhall mention,
Compounded with your own invention,
I'm ſure will anſwer my intention.
Of love take firſt a due proportion—
It ſerves to keep the heart in motion :
Of jealouſy a powerful zeſt,
Of all tormenting paſſions beſt ;
Of horror mix a copious ſhare,
And duels you muſt never ſpare ;

Hyſteric

Hyſteric fits at leaſt a ſcore,

Or, if you find occaſion, more;

But fainting fits you need not meaſure,

The fair ones have them at their pleaſure;

Of ſighs and groans take no account,

But throw them in to vaſt amount;

A frantic fever you may add,

Moſt authors make their lovers mad;

Rack well your hero's nerves and heart,

And let your heroine take her part;

Her fine blue eyes were made to weep,

Nor ſhould ſhe ever taſte of ſleep;

Ply her with terrors day or night,

And keep her always in a fright,

But in a carriage when you get her,

Be ſure you fairly overſet her;

If ſhe will break her bones—why let her:

Again, if e'er ſhe walks abroad,

Of courſe you bring ſome wicked lord,

Who with three ruffians fnaps his prey,
And to a caftle fpeeds away;
There clofe confin'd in haunted tower,
You leave your captive in his power,
Till dead with horror and difmay,
She fcales the walls and flies away.

Now you contrive the lovers meeting,
To fet your reader's heart a beating,
But ere they've had a moment's leifure,
Be fure to interrupt their pleafure;
Provide yourfelf with frefh alarms
To tear 'em from each other's arms;
No matter by what fate they're parted,
So that you keep them broken-hearted.

A cruel father fome prepare
To drag her by her flaxen hair;
Some raife a ftorm, and fome a ghoft,
Take either, which may pleafe you moft.

But

But this you muſt with care obſerve,

That when you've wound up every nerve

With expectation, hope and fear,

Hero and heroine muſt diſappear.

Some fill one book, ſome two without 'em,

And ne'er concern their heads about 'em,

This greatly reſts the writer's brain,

For any ſtory, that gives pain,

You now throw in—no matter what,

However foreign to the plot,

So it but ſerves to ſwell the book,

You foiſt it in with deſperate hook—

A maſquerade, a murder'd peer,

His throat juſt cut from ear to ear—

A rake turn'd hermit—a fond maid

Run mad, by ſome falſe loon betray'd—

Theſe ſtores ſupply the female pen,

Which writes them o'er and o'er again,

And readers likewiſe may be found

To circulate them round and round.

Now

Now at your fable's clofe devife
Some grand event to give furprize—
Suppofe your hero knows no mother—
Suppofe he proves the heroine's brother—
This at one ftroke diffolves each tie,
Far as from eaft to weft they fly:
At length when every woe's expended,
And your laft volume's nearly ended,
Clear the miftake, and introduce
Some tatt'ling nurfe to cut the noofe,
The fpell is broke—again they meet
Expiring at each other's feet;
Their friends lie breathlefs on the floor—
You drop your pen; you can no more—
And ere your reader can recover,
They're married—and your hiftory's over.

THE POWER OF FANCY.

WRITTEN FOR THE VASE AT BATH-EASTON.

FANCY, come !—thou fertile theme,
　And thy choiceſt colours ſpread,
Airy phantom, waking dream,
　Show'r thy odours on my head !

Sweet enchantreſs, tune my lyre,
　Gently place me on thy wing,
Robe me in thy gay attire,
　Whilſt thy power I ſtrive to ſing.

Then thy pinions wide expand,
　Swift purſue thine eagle flight,
Guide me with thy magic wand,
　Bear me paſt the reach of ſight.

Watt

Waft me thro' thofe fragrant gales,
　　Which exhale from Pindus' hill,
Lead me to thofe flowery vales,
　　Water'd by Caftalia's rill.

Give me of that limpid ftream,
　　Which the fportive mufes fip,
So fhould I that draught efteem
　　Sweet as nectar to my lip.

Thence on fam'd Parnaffus' mount,
　　Kind conductrefs, let me light,
There would I thy power recount,
　　If to me thou would'ft indite.

Offering meet I then might bring
　　To the Mufe's fav'rite Vafe,
And to ftrains melodious fing
　　Carols in the Donor's praife.

But

But me, alas ! no mufe infpires,

   Nor fancy aids, nor fylphs indite,

No whifpering gales, nor founding lyre,

   To numbers fweet my pen invite.

Yet tho' no laurels I can claim,

   No plaudits from your circle meet,

Still fhall it be my humble aim

   To lay my offerings at your feet.

THE XXIII^D PSALM.

The Lord is my shepherd, my guardian and guide,
For the wants of his creatures the Lord doth provide;
E'er since I was born it is he that hath crown'd
The life that he gave me with blessings around.
While yet on the breast a poor infant I hung,
Ere time had unloosen'd the strings of my tongue,
He gave me the help which I could not then ask,
And now, oh my tongue, let his praise be thy task!

Thro' my tenderest years, with as tender a care,
My soul like a lamb in his bosom he bare;
To the brook he would lead me whene'er I had need,
And point out the pasture where best I might feed;
No harm would approach me, for he was my shield
From the birds of the air and the beast of the field;

The

The wolf to devour me would often times prowl,
But the Lord was my fhepherd, and guarded my foul.

How oft in my youth have I wandered aftray,
And ftill he hath fet me again on the way;
When loft in dark error no path I could meet,
His word like a lanthorn hath guided my feet ;
What wond'rous efcapes to his kindnefs I owe,
When rafh and unthinking I fought my own woe ;
My foul had long fince been gone down to the deep,
If the Lord had not watched when I was afleep.

Whene'er at a diftance he fees me afraid,
O'er the hills and high mountains he comes to my aid,
Then leads me back gently, and bids me abide
In the midft of his flock, and feed clofe by his fide ;
How happy if there I could ever remain
All the days of my life, and not wander again ;
Yea, bleft are the people, and happy thrice told,
Who obey the Lord's voice and abide in his fold.

The

The fold it is full, and the pasture is green,

All is friendship and love, and no enemy seen ;

There the Lord dwells amongst us upon his own hill,

And the mountains all round with his presence
    doth fill,

Himself in the midst with a provident eye,

Regarding our wants and procuring supply ;

He prepareth all things for our safety and food,

We gather his gifts, and are filled with good.

When he leads forth the flock we all gladly obey

For the Lord is himself both our leader and way,

The hills smoke with incense where e'er he hath trod,

And a sacred perfume shews the footsteps of God,

Whilst blest with his presence the valleys beneath

A sweet smelling favour do constantly breathe ;

He reneweth the face of each living thing,

And the glad Earth enjoys a perpetual spring.

Or if a far different scene he prepare,

And we march thro' the wilderness barren and bare,

By

By his wonderful works we fee plainly enough
That the earth is the Lord's and the fullnefs thereof;
When hungry and thirfty we're ready to faint,
He feeth our need and prevents our complaint;
The rain at his word brings us bread from the fky,
And rocks become rivers when nature is dry.

From the fruitfulleft hill to the barreneft rock
The Lord hath made all for the fake of his flock,
And the flock in return the Lord always confefs,
Their joy in abundance, their hope in diftrefs;
He beholds in our welfare his glory difplay'd,
And we deem ourfelves happy when he is obey'd;
With a cheerful regard we attend to his ways,
Our attention is prayer, and our cheerfulnefs praife.

FROM THE XIITH CHAPTER OF ST. MARK,
41ST VERSE, TO THE END.

═══

Hail, widow! ample caufe haft thou to blefs
That happy ftate, which others term diftrefs,
Since by thy Saviour's voice it is proclaim'd,
That wherefoe'er his gofpel fhall be nam'd,
There fhall recorded ftand thy pious deed,
The mite beftow'd of which thyfelf had need.
Such was thy charity, thy faith, thy love,
The gift was regifter'd in heav'n above.
What tho' the rich, whofe coffers overflow'd,
With oftentation their vain alms beftow'd,
'Twas but a part from that abundance given,
Which they as almoners receiv'd from heaven,
Thou from thine all with confidence didft part,
Unknown to thee, thy Saviour faw thy heart.

H Y M N.

To thee, all powerful and fupreme,
   I tune my grateful lays,
When fuch, and fo divine, the theme,
   How weak is mortal praife!

Yet pardon, if in humble verfe
   My' enraptur'd foul afpire,
Thy wond'rous goodnefs to rehearfe,
   Thy greatnefs to admire.

Let my o'erflowing heart difcharge
   In prayer and praife to thee
Some fmall return for gifts fo large
   Beftow'd each day on me.

Ah, what am I, that thou fhould'ft deign
　To vifit my fad heart?
And why vouchfafe, when I complain,
　Such folace to impart?

'Tis in the words of life I meet
　A cure for every grief,
'Tis ever to thy mercy-feat
　I fly to feek relief.

I find it there, I feel a flame
　Within my bofom glow,
I call upon my Saviour's name,
　And triumph over woe.

Vain is the world's unkindnefs, vain
　Misfortune's utmoft fpite,
Whilft ftill I keep 'midft grief and pain
　Thy mercies in my fight.

　　　　I know

I know that my Redeemer lives,

    I know that He can fave,

Let Him take back the life he gives,

    I'll feek Him in the grave.

TO A CERTAIN AUTHOR,

ON HIS

WRITING A PROLOGUE,

WHEREIN HE DESCRIBES A TRAVELLER FROZEN IN A SNOW

STORM.

No more let poets vainly boaſt
   Their fine deſcriptive art,
They ranſack Nature's gayeſt ſtore,
   Yet rarely warm the heart.

Hail, happy Bard, whoſe brilliant wit,
   With more than Poet's art,
Can from a frozen maſs extract
   Fire that can melt the heart.

IN RETURN FOR THE PRESENT OF A
PAIR OF BUCKLES.

———

The female heart by bribes is oft affail'd,
 Full oft by bribes the female heart is won,
When tears, and fighs, and flatteries have fail'd,
 An ear ring or a necklace might have done.

Hence men their court by various prefents make,
 A fong, a fan, a top-knot, or a glove,
The gift, ftill pleafing for the giver's fake,
 Is welcom'd as an emblem of his love.

My gentle fwain a happier art has found
 At once his paffion and fuccefs to prove,
Whilft by his magic gift my feet are bound,
 No power is left me to efcape his love.

THE AIR BALLOON.

No more of Phaeton let poets tell,
I care not where he drove nor where he fell;
No more I'll wish for fam'd Aurora's car,
To drive me forth, high as the morning star;
In Air Balloon to distant realms I go,
" And leave the gazing multitude below."

No more I'll hear of Venus and her doves,
Nor Cupid flying with the little loves;
Nor would I now in Juno's chariot ride
In princely pomp, with peacock by my side;
In higher state, in Air Balloon I go,
I'd have the gods and goddesses to know.

No more in oriental language fair
I'll read of Genii wafting through the air;

Nor

Nor longer will I feek (by Perfian wrought)
A carpet, to tranfport me by a thought;
Enough for me in Air Balloon to go,
And leave th' enquiring multitude below.

No more of Pegafus (unruly fteed)
To reach Parnaffus' Mount, fhall I have need;
Nor will I now the Mufes favour court,
To fhew me Pindus' Hill, their chief refort;
To thefe fair realms in Air Balloon I go,
And leave the grov'ling multitude below.

No more fhall Fancy now (betwitching fair!)
Erect me caftles, floating in the air;
Such vague, fuch feeble ftructures I defpife,
I'll kick them down as I afcend the fkies;
For higher far in Air Balloon I go,
And leave the wond'ring multitude below.

No longer, now, at diftance need I try
To trace each planet with perfpective eye;

Nor longer wifh, with fairies from afar,

To flide me gently down on falling ftar;

For up or down with equal eafe I fteer,

And view with naked eye the fplendid fphere.

Alas poor Newton ! late for learning fam'd,

No more fhall thy refearches e'er be nam'd;

For greater Newtons now each day fhall foar,

High up to Heaven, and new worlds explore;

Since fwift, in Air Balloons, aloft we go,

And leave the ftupid multitude below.

No more the terrors of the deep I fear;

Alike to me, if friend be far or near;

This fea-girt ifle I diftant leave behind,

Vifit each kingdom and furvey mankind;

For now with cafe in Air Balloon I ride,

No more compell'd to wait for wind or tide.

Hail, happy lovers ! late by diflance curft,

(Of all the worldly tortures fure the worft)

No more condemn'd an abfence to deplore,
And, fighing, breathe your vows from fhore to fhore;
For through the air, fwift in Balloons ye roll,
" And waft yourfelves from India to the pole."

In vain may party rage affail mine ear;
If war or peace, alike I'm free from care;
Should plague or peftilence infect the land,
The pureft regions are at my command;
Where fafe from harm, in Air Balloon I go,
And leave the fickly multitude below.

No more of judge or jury will I hear,
The laws of land extend not to the air;
Nor bailiff now my fpirits can affright,
For up I mount, and foon am out of fight;
Thus, fcreen'd from juftice, in Balloon I go,
And leave th' infolvent multitude below.

How few the worldly evils now I dread,
No more confin'd this narrow earth to tread:

Should

Should fire, or water, fpread deftruction drear,

Or earthquake fhake this fublunary fphere,

In Air Balloon to diftant realms I fly,

And leave the creeping world to fink and die.

THE LXIIIᴅ PSALM.

———

O God, thou art my only God,
   My Saviour and my King,
Early thy face, O Lord, I feek,
   Thy praife I ftrive to fing.

My fainting foul, when parch'd with thirft,
   To thee looks up for aid ;
My wearied flefh by barren lands
   And drought is fore difmay'd.

Thus have I fought my heav'nly King
   In holinefs to fee ;
Oh, let my foul confefs thy power,
   And glory ftill in thee.

Far better than the life itſelf
   Thy kindneſs do I prize,
My lips thy praiſes ſhall rehearſe
   For ever on this wiſe.

For ever magnify my God,
   And ſtill record his fame,
My hands while I have life, lift up
   In honour of his name,

Thus ſhall my ſoul be ſatisfied,
   Even as with daintieſt meat,
When I with joyful lips thy praiſe
   For evermore repeat.

HYMN.

The Lord is my shepherd, what then shall I fear?
What danger can frighten me whilst he is near?
Not when the day comes that I pass thro' the Vale
Of the Shadow of Death, shall my heart ever fail.
Tho' afraid by myself to pursue the dark way,
Thy rod and thy staff are my comfort and stay;
For I know by thy guidance, when once it is past,
To a fountain of life it will lead me at last.

The Lord is become my salvation and song,
His blessings shall follow me all my life long;
Whatever condition he places me in,
I know 'tis the best it could ever have been,
For the Lord he is good and his mercies are sure,
He only afflicteth in order to cure;
The Lord will I praise whilst I have any breath,
Be content all my life, and resign'd at my death.

A COLLEGE LIFE.

FOR THE VASE AT BATH-EASTON.

A COLLEGE life! I fcorn the odious phrafe;
So dull a theme fhall ne'er employ my lays:
A life indeed! 'twere fitter ftil'd a death,
Unlefs 'tis life merely to draw your breath;
By fufty walls coop'd up, as in a pen,
'Mongft fufty books, and ftill more fufty men.
Can this be life, by gothic rules compell'd
To part from liberty, or be expell'd?
At early dawn roufed by the bell to matin,
The live long day confined to Greek and Latin;
At fuch an hour amongft old dons to dine,
Yet not allow'd a focial glafs of wine;
With cap in hand acrofs the court to go,
But not to touch the grafs-plat with your toe,

Left

Left dire expulsion for that breach of laws

Seize on the culprit with it's iron claws.

If when fatigu'd at ev'ning, he should take

A nap too long, and not to pray'rs awake,

Strait through the College shall his name resound,

Dead or alive, the caitiff must be found:

Or if perchance some friend or lady fair

Should draw him forth to taste the noontide air,

Then as a squirrel, who his chain has broke,

Or slave new ranfom'd from his galling yoke,

His liberty he hugs, with joy elate,

He for a while forgets his servile state, }

Nor e'er reflects on bars, or keys, or gate.

But now the college clock with gloomy knell

Affails his ear, and like conjurer's spell

Strikes thro' his heart —with horror in his face

Sudden he starts—his short-liv'd joy gives place.

With eager strides swift thro' the streets he hies,

And at the portal for admittance cries,

But cries in vain—for ah! 'tis all too late;

The porter hears, but won't unbar the gate;

Abash'd

Abaſh'd the youth retires with thoughful pace,
Dreams of jobation, lectures and diſgrace;
Next morn by Maſter, Tutor, Fellows rated,
In ſhort, not much unlike a bear when baited.

Since this a College Life, peace to that pair,
Who dying left me to a Guardian's care,
And he, thank Fortune, to unbend my mind,
Choſe a young Tutor, gay, polite and kind,
Who, anxious much my morals to advance,
Took me a tour thro' Italy and France;
Gave me the Graces, which I more admire
Than all the learning I could elſe acquire:
This, this is life, but that within a College,
Which muſty pedants term the Seat of Knowledge,
Let pedants take—I will not ſee their faces,
But live and die devoted to the Graces.

Thus Florio talk'd—much noiſe and little matter,
'Tis thus, that puppies yelp, and monkies chatter.

ON THE VIOLENT DEBATES

IN THE

HOUSE OF PEERS,

UPON THE BILL FOR SUSPENDING THE HABEAS CORPUS, &c.

My noble Lords, your altercation
Can never tend to ferve the nation,
  You can't but know its laws ;
Why then, right noble Peers, this pother,
As if each culprit were your brother,
  That thus you plead their caufe ?

Prythee, my Lords, be quiet then,
Strive to acquit yourfelves like men,
  Who hold a facred truft ;
Your Church, your King, your Country calls
For unity within your walls,
  For meafures firm and juft.

EPIGRAM.

===

Why will you, W * *, feek with *Paine* to find
Men like yourfelves of difcontented mind ?
Believe me, Sir, you may as well be quiet,
Do what you will, you cannot hatch a riot ;
If Reformation 's all you wifh to get,
Reform yourfelf, and leave the State to Pitt.

A PARODY

UPON

WHO DARES TO KILL KILDARE.

Who dares appear t' appoint Pierpoint a Peer?
  The bufy Faction cries—
I dare appear t' appoint Pierpoint a Peer,
  The Minifter replies.

A PARODY

UPON

SWIFT's NURSES' SONG.

———

On my Charley, my Charley,
The man of the people was he;
Such a sweet pet as Charley
No one did ever see.

" Once he went up, up, uppy,
" Long he's gone down, down, downy,
" Oft he's gone backwards and forwards,
" And now he's quite run agrouney."

Has

Has he loft all his credit,
And has he loft all his money?
His friends will all make him a purfe,
For he's ftill their own dear honey.

        " Once he went up, &c."

Here are his own two Dukies,
Each with his thoufand in handey;
Here are three Earls and a Marquis,
And here is his dear Napper Tandy.

        " Once he went up, &c."

Earl S————pe, as ftraight as a fteeple,
On the table puts down his five poundy,
Then drinks to the Man of the People,
And the glafs it goes merrily roundy.

        " Once he went up, &c."

Next comes his own dear Sh————ry,
No friend like to Sh————ry on earth,
A thoufand good pounds he fubfcribes,
Which is more than poor Sh————ry is worth.

      " Once he went up, &c."

Then be not difcourag'd, dear Charley,
Your friends are all met in convention,
Contented to lofe their own credit,
By fixing on you a good penfion.

" Once he went up, up, uppy,
" Long he's gone down, down, downy,
" Oft he's gone backwards and forwards,
" And now he's quite run agrouney."

RIDDLE.

I TOOK five daughters with me to the play,
The firſt in *ſcarlet* clad, the next in *grey*,
In *ſilk* the third, the fourth in *gold* array'd,
In humble *ſtuff* the laſt, and youngeſt maid.

DITTO.

I HAVE five ſons, I tell it you in grief,
And each of them a *cut-throat* or a *thief*.

CHARADE.

My firſt has exalted the heroes of old,

 My ſecond's the teſt of a ſhrew,

My whole is ſo mean, to it's ſhame be it told,

 It will crouch to the ſole of your ſhoe.

DITTO.

My firſt for temper and for tongue

 Is to a proverb curſt ;

My ſecond is for ever hung

 By nature to my firſt.

When drawling periods without end

 Exhauſt the hearer's ſoul,

To Parſon Spintext, as a friend,

 I recommend my whole.

D I T T O.

To a term oft made ufe of by partners in trade
Add a pious young damfel for ever a maid,
With five hundred tackt to a fpirituous liquor,
Which is drank from the cobler quite up to the vicar,
Thefe, when right put together, will quickly explain
The name of a thing made to puzzle the brain.

UPON READING SOME VERSES UPON A SCULL.

———

And are we thus transformed by fate?
Is this the fhape each face muft wear?
Well might'ft thou paint that final ftate,
Thy purity can never fear.

Yet let my foul furvey the grace,
The fafhion of her fair abode,
There thro' the wond'rous fabrick trace
The finger of unerring God.

Who bade the blood in equal round
I.'s vital warmth throughout difpenfe?
Who tun'd the ear for every found?
Who lent the hand its ready fenfe?

Whence

Whence had the eye its fubtle force,
The vifual and enlight'ning ray ?
Who tun'd the lips with prompt difcourfe,
And whence the foft and honey'd lay ?

Yes, thy Creator's image there
In each expreffive part is feen,
But thine immortal part doth bear
That image pictur'd beft within.

Elfe what availed the enraptured ftrain,
Did not the mind her aid impart ?
The melting eye might fpeak in vain,
Flow'd not it's language from the heart.

The blood in ftated pace had crept
Along the dull and fluggifh veins,
The ear infenfibly had flept,
'Tho' angels fung in choiceft ftrains.

No victor laurel had been feen
Upon the brow of glorious war,
The regulated fight had been
A cafual, blind, tumultuous jar,

Know, 'tis the foul, the work of heaven,
That fets the proper ftamp on all;
According to the freedom given,
The man, when judg'd, fhall ftand or fall,

Nor fhall this habitation frail
The active fpirit content alone,
Wond'ring it fcans the mighty fcale,
Which links the whole creation one,

Strong and extenfive in it's view,
It launches midft the boundlefs fky,
Sees planets other orbs purfue,
Whofe fyftems other funs fupply,

Blufh

Blush then, if thou haft fenfe of fhame,
Inglorious, ignorant, impious flave,
Who think'ft this heaven-created frame
Shall bafely perifh in the grave!

Falfe as thou art, dar'ft thou fuggeft
That the Almighty is unjuft?
Wilt thou the truth with him conteft,
Whofe wifdom form'd thee from the duft?

Say, dotard, hath he idly wrought,
Or are his works to be believed?
Speak! is the whole creation nought?
Mortal! is God, or thou, deceived?

Thy harden'd fpirit convict at laft
It's damned error fhall perceive,
Speechlefs fhall hear it's fentence pafs'd,
Condemn'd to tremble and believe.

But thou, in Reason's sober light,
Death clad with terrors canst survey
And from that foul and ghastly sight
Derive the pure and moral ray.

Go on, sweet nymph, in virtue's course,
So shall the tomb corrupt and vile,
The shades of darkness lose their force,
The distant frown become a smile.

And when the neceffary day
Shall call thee to thy saving God,
Secure, thou'lt chuse that better way,
Which none but faints like thee have trod.

Thus shall thy foul at length forsake
The sweetest form e'er foul receiv'd,
Of those rich bleffings to partake
Which eye ne'er saw, nor heart conceiv'd.

There,

There, midft the full angelic throng,

Praife him who thofe rich bleffings gave;

There fhall refume the grateful fong,

‘ A joyful victor o’er the grave.’

WRITTEN AT SWANDLING BAR,

IN THE COUNTY OF CAVAN, IN IRELAND.

═══

Let thofe who would efteem it good
  To reach the age of Par,
By water pure come and infure
  Their lives at Swandling Bar.

Let all who be, by land or fea,
  However near or far,
Make no delay, but hafte away,
  To drink at Swandling Bar.

Should belle or beau the fcurvy fhow,
  Which doth all beauty mar,
Hither repair, you'll foon grow fair,
  When once at Swandling Bar.

Each

Each goddefs here, tho' now fo clear,
　　Shew'd like a fallen ftar,
When firft from town fhe pofted down
　　To drink at Swandling Bar.

Each fot and rake his cure might make,
　　And wage with Death a war,
Would he but think the beft of drink
　　Is that at Swandling Bar.

Oft have I feen, come to careen,
　　Many an honeft tar,
With batter'd hide by fcurvy dried,
　　Yet cur'd at Swandling Bar.

I've feen a fair who might compare,
　　With Venus in her car,
Approach the rill and drink her fill
　　Each day at Swandling Bar.

Here

Here lords from town, of high renown,
    With garter and with ſtar,
Decrepid come, yet briſk go home,
    Such power hath Swandling Bar.

Late have I ſeen, of graceful mien,
    A nymph from Mullingar,
So fair, ſo bright, ſhe caught the ſight
    Of all at Swandling Bar.

Tho' here I came to quench a flame
    I've got a deeper ſcar,
Yet can't endure to ſeek a cure
    By leaving Swandling Bar.

A SONG.

TO THE TUNE OF, YE BELLES AND YE FLIRTS.

———

Y E fleerers and flirts, and ye *proud little* things,
    When receiv'd by your neighbours around,
Pri'thee tell me from whence your impertinence fprings,
    Good manners at once to confound?
What means the fly wink, the fatyrical fneer,
    The whifper that wounds as it flies?
Poor girls, ye have fadly miftaken, I fear,
    Both the ufe of your tongue, and your eyes.
              Poor girls, &c.

The blufh of the rofe and the mildnefs of morn
    Are beauties no art can fupply;
By nature, they're yours, and 'tis you they adorn,
    In your cheek, in your lip, in your eye.
                 But

But if traitors to Nature, their virtue you flight,
   And put Malice and Art in their place,
Both Cupid and Hymen you'll foon put to flight,
   And *quiz* away every Grace.

              Poor girls, &c.

The nymph who on beauty and fatire depends,
   Muft call all her wits to her aid,
Which fhe greatly will need, when fhe's loft all her
     friends,
   And is left a forfaken old maid.
Whilft the fair one, whofe fenfe and good nature
     fhe try'd,
   In the days of her frolic and fport,
Is now far above her, and but for her pride,
   She gladly her favour would court.

              Poor girls, &c.

                   Thofe

Those virtues, and charms, which we prize in the fair,

 Alas! are neglected by you :

Humility pines, and good sense in despair

 Has totally bid you adieu.

Yet recal your lost reason, and banish your pride,

 And what charms you possess we'll approve ;

If adorn'd with those merits, which now you deride,

 You'll regain our esteem and our love.

     Dear girls, &c.

A PARTY AT QUADRILLE.

LADY POOLE'S HOUSE.

Enter Lady WRANGLE, Mrs. FRETT, *and* Mr. CARDER.

Lady P. LADIES, your fervant, this indeed is kind
 To come to one fo much diftrefs'd in mind ;
 Since Friday laft, the day poor Pompey died,
 No foul I've feen, nor left my fire-fide.
Lady W. Well, deareft Madam, talk no more of that,
 Nothing is like a game at cards, and chat,
 To eafe the mind ; I'm fure I found it fo
 When poor Sir Simon died ; you all well know
 How very much reliev'd I was by play ;
 When morn was over I began the day.

Mr.

Mr. C.   Come ladies, then 'tis beſt to loſe no time,
  To dwell on griefs I always deem a crime.

Lady P.   Pray, ladies, take your places as you chuſe;
  In every ſeat I know I'm ſure to loſe.

Mrs. F.   To loſe! dear Ma'am, *I* think to leave off play,
  Such cards *I* ſat with all the other day,
  When in this very houſe your La'ſhip won;
  'Tis what I never do, I've ſuch a run.
  Beaſted ſuch hands! I loſt on Tueſday night
  Three double mattadores, they broke me quite.

Lady P.   Ladies, your ſtakes. We play our uſual rate.

Mrs. F.   Here, Madam's, mine; 'tis gone as ſure as fate.

Lady P.   Sir, you have paſs'd, I now may ſhew my cards;
  Six mattadores; four fiſh are my reward.

Lady W.   Indeed! this way the cards are ſure to go,
  Whatever game I play, or high or low.
  The other night I loſt at Lady Vole's
  My twenty ſhillings, now at Lady Poole's
  This night I'm like to loſe three times that ſum;
  I ſwear I'll keep from Mrs. Fuzz's drum.

         Mrs.

Mrs. F.   I take a king if no one plays alòne.

Lady W.   *Madam, I do*; I'll not fit like a drone

With mattadores, fix trumps; 'tis monftrous hard

To have a vole within one fingle card.

Might I have took a king. I'd had it clear,

But fome folks cards will always play fevere.

Mrs. F. Severe indeed ! Sure mine the hardeft cafe is,

To fit thus long, and never fee the aces.

And now, the firft time I could take a king,

I'm fuperfeded, that's the very thing.

I fometimes get a hand, but never play ;

I owe your La'fhip four, I've none to pay.

Lady P.   I'll mark you up, dear Ma'am, the ufual

way.

Mrs. F.   Well, now by chance at laft I've got a game,

And if you all give leave, my trump I'll name ;

Hearts then it is; fpadille I lead, oh fie !

One hand without a trump ! how hard they lie.

Lady P. Madam, you have your game, no trump is in,

Mrs. F. Yes, Ma'am, becaufe this hand of courfe muft

win.

Lady P.   Upon my honour, now, I've never play'd
But one poor hand, and now fix fifh have paid.
I vow next time I deal I'll make a fuz.

Mrs. F. I wonder how your next door neighbour does
I heard laft week he loft his only fon.

Lady P.   Yes, and his wife is dying. What is done?
I think your La'fhip afk'd? I pafs of courfe;
Upon my life my cards get worfe and worfe.

Mrs. F. I'm quite fupriz'd, I'm really call'd this time,
It is your La'fhip's trick, 'tis none of mine;
For if not call'd I'd been a bitter foe.
Let's fee thofe cards, I know not how they go.

Mr. C.   Ladies, I think the vole's at your command,
At leaft I can't prevent it by my hand.

Lady W.   Ma'am, you're to fpeak; pray fearch the
tricks again.

Mrs. F.   My deareft Ma'am, I fear 'tis all in vain,
One fatal chance would overfet the whole;
And yet 'twould make us both to win a vole.
Can you forgive me? May I now declare.

Lady P   Madam, proceed; this is not quite fo fair.

Lady W. Oh, Mrs. Frett, you've ruin'd me indeed;

    How could it e'er be won, and you to lead?

    My Lady Poole did well to bid us play

    When she'd that knave; we've all the world to pay.

Mrs. F.   Indeed, I think so too; she drew me in;

    Yet sure the chance was great that we should win.

Lady W.   By no means, Ma'am; your play I can't

        excuse;

    I'm sadly wrong'd, for I could not refuse.

Lady P. Well, Ladies, please to lay your money down,

    The pool's my constant care, 'tis always known;

    I'm sure you'd mattadores, so give us five;

    Now this may turn my luck, and I may thrive.

    Poor Mr. Carder was without a fish,

    But now he's rich, and just as he could wish.

Lady W.   I know not who is rich, I'm sure I'm poor,

    And lay my ruin at that Lady's door.

Mrs. F, Indeed, dear Ma'am, you see I'm quite undone;

    'Tis very hard to twit, when if we'd won

    You'd been the first to justify my play;

    But let it pass your Ladyship's own way;

                  This

This fine lone hand fome of my debts will fettle;

'Tis but my due to *ride on my own cattle.*

Lady W. 'Tis very lucky, Mrs. Fret, for you,

But with thefe lofies what am I to do?

I wifh with all my heart the pool was out,

For I'm engag'd to Lady Racket's rout.

Lady P. That's quite diftreffing, Ma'am, but I fubmit;

'Twill break our fet ; but juft as you think fit.

The pool is out, upon my word I win.

Lady W. Indeed, I thought your La'fhip's pawn was in.

Lady P. Oh no, I took that out an hour ago ;

I'm fure, Sir, you will witnefs it was fo.

Mr. C. Madam, I always think your La'fhip right ;

I juft have loft three guineas by the night.

Lady P. O lack-a-day ! 'twas unpolite to beat

Our only man—'twas an unlucky feat.

We've won an even fhare, or very nigh.

The cards to-night have not run very high.

Ladies, your humble fervant, Sir, good bye.

WRITTEN FROM BATH TO A FRIEND IN
THE COUNTRY, IN THE YEAR 1785.

WHAT! breathe *Anstean* air, and yet not send
One ambling rhyme to my sequester'd friend;
Forbid it every Muse of Avon's stream,
(Apollo's chief resort, if right I deem);
And you, ye Nine, which o'er Batheaston's urn
Preside, to give the *myrtle* wreath, *or burn*;
Who at the call of many a daring wight,
Who ne'er before in verse essay'd to write,
Attendant fly, impregnating the air
With Ode and Sonnet to the blooming fair,
To me, your suppliant, deign to waft a breeze
From Avon's banks, and fam'd Batheaston's trees:
Thus borne aloft Parnassus Hill I'll climb,
And write my Journal in *Anstean rhyme*.

I.   So

So firſt taking in a great gulp of the air,
And trying to find the poetical chair,
To tell you my hiſt'ry with ſpeed I prepare.

For ſurely 'tis right my relations ſhould know it,
That their wandering couſin is turn'd out a poet;
Ah, well would it be, ſince this place is ſo dear,
Could ſhe turn a camelion, and live on the air,
Or like poets of old, to a garret retire,
And ne'er to a hall or a parlour aſpire;
For, ſtrange to relate it, there's not to be found
Two rooms by the year under *fifty good pound*;
But ſince 'tis the faſhion to ſpend all one's worth,
'Tis beſt to beſtow it on pleaſure and mirth,
So at Bath will I live, let it end as it may,
And a lodging I'll take in the ſtreet titled Gay.
But how to deſcribe the fine ſights which I ſee,
Or the Lady *Bab Frightfuls*, who drink up my tea,
With all their fine ſpeeches to me and my friend,
With the tickets for balls, or the notes which they ſend,

For

For all fo polite are, fo civil and kind,

That to tell you the half on't no words can I find;

Nor muft I omit how the mornings glide on,

For I'm told to wafte time is entirely the ton,

So I'm fure I am right in the method I take,

For l wafte all my time from the hour I awake;

For what more can do it, than breakfafting out,

And then in the ftreet to go ftrolling about,

Then ftep to the Painters to reft me a while,

Acquaintance to meet, and the hours to beguile,

Or elfe to the Pump-room, by way of a frolic,

To drink of the waters, which give me the cholic;

But I'm told at this place 'tis genteel to be ill, ⎫

So I've got my good *landlord* to give me a pill, ⎬

And to add a few draughts to make up a bill. ⎭

Then home to my dinner with fpeed I repair,

Which quickly is o'er, then to dreffing my hair;

For who can appear in a place fo polite,

Unlefs on the head each hair ftands upright;

Or

Or who in a circle is fit to be feen
Unlefs drefs'd as young as if barely fifteen.
This bufinefs when ended with trouble and care,
Without lofs of time I get into my chair,
And ftraight to the Ball-room or Play-houfe I hafte,
For vifits of friendfhip are quite out of tafte;
Nay, I'm told it is vulgar beyond all compare
To own a relation, tho' ever fo near.

But what pen can defcribe the high heads I behold,
Not tired like the matrons we read of, when old;
No, thefe pretty creatures are juft the reverfe,
And their heads at a diftance appear like a hearfe,
With plumes fweetly nodding, with plaits and with
    gold,
With things out of number which ne'er can be told,
Which ferve to convince me St. Peter's not read
By folks of *high tafte*, who are *perfectly bred*;
And I can't but believe that they pafs all the morning
In learning to dance, and their heads thus adorning.

                Oh.

Oh, were you to fee the fine capers they give,

You ne'er would forget it as long as you live;

But I cannot relate you the half that I fee,

Nor how we eat cake, or how we drink tea,

For the clock has ftruck fix, and the poft's at the
    door;

But if this fhould delight you, you foon fhall have
    more.

EXTRACTS FROM ECCLESIASTICUS,

COMPILED TOGETHER ON VARIOUS SUBJECTS.

———

ON WISDOM.

ALL wifdom cometh from the Lord, and is with him for ever.

Wifdom hath been created before all things, and the underftanding of prudence from everlafting.

The word of God moft high is the fountain of wifdom, and her ways are everlafting commandments.

To whom hath the knowledge of wifdom been made manifeft ? and who hath underftood her great experience ?

To whom hath the root of wifdom been made known, or to whom hath her wife counfels been revealed ?

There is one wife, and greatly to be feared, the Lord fitting upon his throne.

He

He created, and faw her, and numbered her, and poured her out on all his works.

She is with all flefh, according to her gift, and he hath given her to thofe that love him.

She hath built an everlafting habitation with men, and fhe fhall continue with their feed.

She filleth all their houfes with things defirable, and their garners with her increafe.

Wifdom raineth down fkill, and knowledge of underftanding, and exalteth them to honour that hold her faft.

The root of wifdom is to fear the Lord, and the branches thereof are long life.

If thou defire wifdom, keep the commandments, and the Lord fhall give her to thee.

Wifdom exalteth her children, and layeth hold of them that feek her.

He that loveth her, loveth life, and they that feek her early, fhall be filled with joy.

They that ferve her fhall minifter to the Holy One, and thofe that love her the Lord doth love.

Whofo giveth ear to her fhall judge the nations, and he that attendeth to her fhall dwell fecurely.

My

My fon, gather wifdom from thy youth up, fo fhalt thou find her till thine old age.

Come unto her as to one that plougheth and foweth, and wait for her good fruits, for thou fhalt not toil much in labouring about her, but thou fhalt eat of her fruits right foon.

Bow down thy fhoulder, and bear her, and be not grieved with her **bonds**.

Come unto her with **thy** whole heart, and keep her ways with all thy power.

For at the laft thou fhalt find her reft, and that fhall be turned to thy joy.

Then fhall her fetters be a ftrong defence for thee, and her chains a robe of glory.

For there is a golden ornament upon her, and her bands are purple lace.

Thou fhalt put her on as a robe of honour, and fhall put her about thee as a crown of joy.

Bleffed is the man that doth meditate good things in wifdom, and that reafoneth of holy things by his underftanding; he fhall pitch his tent nigh unto her, and fhall lodge in a lodging where good things are; he fhall fet his children under her fhelter, and they fhall lodge under her branches; by her he fhall be covered from heat, and in her glory fhall he dwell; with the bread of underftanding

ing fhall fhe feed, and give him the water of wifdom to drink; he fhall be ftayed upon her, and
fhall not be moved; he fhall rely upon her, and
fhall not be confounded; fhe fhall exalt him above
his neighbours, and in the midft of the congrega-
tion fhall fhe open his mouth; he fhall find joy
and a crown of gladnefs, and fhe fhall caufe him to
inherit an everlafting name.

Wifdom fhall praife herfelf, and fhall thus glory
in the midft of her people: I came out of the
mouth of the moft high, and covered the earth as
a cloud; I dwelt in high places, and my throne
was in a cloudy pillar; I alone compaffed the cir-
cuit of heaven, and walked in the bottom of the
fea, and in all the earth; in every people and nation I got a poffeffion; for the Creator of all
things gave me a commandment, and he that made
me caufed my tabernacle to reft, and faid, let thy
dwelling be in Jacob, and thine inheritance in If-
rael. In the holy tabernacle I ferved before him,
and fo was I eftablifhed in Sion; likewife in the
beloved city he gave me reft, and in Jerufalem was
my power fixed. I took root in an honourable
people, even in the portion of the Lord's inheritance. I was exalted like a cedar in Lebanus, and
as a cyprefs tree upon the mountains of Hermon;
like a palm tree in Engaddi, and as a rofe tree in
Jericho; as a fair olive tree in a pleafant field, and
as a plane tree by the water. I gave a fweet fcent
like cinnamon and afpalathus. I yielded an odour
like

like the beſt myrrh, as galbanum and onyx, as ſweet
ſtorax, and as the fumes of frankincenſe in the tabernacle. As the turpentine tree I ſtretched out
my branches, and my branches are the branches of
honour and grace; as the vine brought I forth
fruit, and my bloſſoms are thoſe of honour and
riches. I am the mother of fair love and fear, of
knowledge and holy hope; I therefore, being eternal,
am given to all my children, which are named of
him. Come unto me, all ye that labour and are
deſirous of me, and fill yourſelves with my fruits;
for my memorial is ſweeter than honey, and mine
inheritance than the honey-comb; they that eat
me ſhall yet be hungry, and they that drink me
ſhall yet be thirſty.

ON THE FEAR OF THE LORD.

THE fear of the Lord is honour, glory, gladnefs, and a crown of rejoicing. The fear of the Lord maketh a merry countenance, and giveth joy, and gladnefs, and a long life. To fear the Lord is the beginning of wifdom, and it was created with the faithful in the womb. Whofo feareth the Lord, it fhall go well with him at the laft, and he fhall find favour in the day of his death. The fear of the Lord is a crown of wifdom, making peace and perfect health to flourifh, which are the gifts of God, who enlarges the rejoicing of thofe that love him. The fear of the Lord driveth away fins, and when it is prefent it turneth away wrath. The fear of the Lord is wifdom and inftruction, and faith and meeknefs are his delight. Ye that fear the Lord, wait for his mercy, and go not afide, left ye fall; ye that fear the Lord, believe in him, and your reward fhall not fail; ye that fear the Lord, hope for good, and for everlafting joy and mercy. Look at the generations of old, and fee, did ever any truft in the Lord and were confounded; or did any abide in his fear, and were forfaken; or whom

did

did he ever defpife who called upon him? They that fear the Lord will not difobey his word, and they that love him will keep his ways, and will prepare their hearts, and humble their fouls in his fight, faying, we will fall into the hands of the Lord, and not into the hands of man, for as his majefty is, fo is his mercy.

The fear of the Lord is all wifdom, and all wifdom is the performance of the law and the knowledge of his omnipotency. Whofo feareth the Lord will receive his difcipline, and they that feek him early fhall find favour; there fhall no harm happen unto him that feareth the Lord, but in temptation even again will he deliver him; he fhall not be afraid, for the Lord is his hope. Bleffed is the foul of him that feareth the Lord; to whom doth he look? and who is his ftrength? The eyes of the Lord are upon them that fear him; he is their mighty protection and ftrong ftay; a defence from heat, and a cover from the fun at noon; a prefervation from ftumbling, and a help from falling; he raifeth up the foul, and lighteth the eyes; he giveth health, life, and bleffing.

ON DUTY FROM CHILDREN TO
THEIR PARENTS.

———

HEAR me your Father, O ye children, and there-
after that ye may be fafe ; for the Lord hath given
the father honour over the children, and hath con-
firmed the authority of the mother over her fons.
Whofo honoureth his father, maketh an atone-
ment for his fins ; he that honoureth his mother, is
one who layeth up treafure. Whofo honoureth his
father fhall have joy of his own children, and when
he maketh his prayer, it fhall be heard. He that
is dutiful to his father fhall have a long life, and he
that is obedient to his mother, is beloved of the
Lord. He that feareth the Lord will honour his
father, and will do fervice to his parents, as to his
mafters. Honour thy father and thy mother, both
in word and deed, that a bleffing may come upon
thee from them ; for the bleffing of the father efta-
blifhes the houfes of children, but the curfe of the
mother rooteth out foundation.

My fon, help thy father in his age, and grieve
him not as long as he liveth ; and if his underftanding

ing fail, have patience with him, and defpife him not when thou art in thy full ftrength; for the reliev- ing of thy father fhall not be forgotten; in the day of affliction it fhall be remembered; thy fins alfo fhall melt away as the ice in fair warm weather. Honour thy father with thy whole heart, and forget not the forrows of thy mother; remember that thou waft begotten of them, and how can'ft thou recom- penfe them the things they have done for thee? He that forfaketh his father is a blafphemer, and he that angereth his mother is curfed of God.

ON THE DUTY OF PARENTS TO THEIR CHILDREN.

———

Hast thou children? inftruct them, and bow down their neck from their youth. He that loveth his fon caufeth him often to feel the rod, that he may have joy of him in the end; he that chaftifeth his fon fhall have joy in him, and rejoice becaufe of him amongft his acquaintance. Though his father die, yet is he as though he were not dead; for he hath left one behind him that is like himfelf. Whilft he lived, he faw and rejoiced in him, and when he died, he was not forrowful; he left behind him an avenger againft his enemies, and one that fhall requite kindnefs to his friends. He that maketh too much of his fon, fhall bind up his wounds, and his bowels will be troubled at every cry: humour thy child, and he fhall make thee afraid; play with him, and he fhall bring thee to heavinefs; laugh not with him, left thou have forrow with him, and left thou gnafh thy teeth in the end; give him not too much liberty in his youth, and wink not at his follies. Bow down his neck
whilft

whilft he is young, left he wax ftubborn, and be
difobedient to thee, and fo bring forrow to thine
heart.   An horfe not broken becometh headftrong,
and a child left to himfelf will be wilful.

Haft thou daughters? have a care of them ; the
father waketh for his daughter when no man know-
eth, and his care for her taketh away fleep ; when
fhe is young, left fhe pafs the flower of her age, and
being married, left fhe fhould be hated. Keep a fure
watch over a fhamelefs daughter, left fhe make thee
a laughing-ftock to thine enemies, and a bye-word
in the city; a reproach amongft the people, and
make thee afhamed before the multitude.

Marry thy daughter, and thou fhalt have per-
formed a weighty matter; but give her to a man
of underftanding.

An evil nurtured fon is the difhonour of his father that begat him, and a foolifh daughter is born
to his lofs. A wife daughter fhall bring an inheritance to her hufband; but fhe that liveth difho-
neftly is her father's heavinefs. She that is bold,
difhonoureth both her hufband and father, and they
fhall both defpife her.

ON A GOOD WIFE.

BLESSED is the man that hath a virtuous wife, for the number of his days fhall be double; a virtuous woman rejoiceth her hufband, and he fhall fulfil the years of his life in peace.

The grace of a wife delighteth her hufband, and her difcretion will fatten his bones. A fhamefaced and faithful woman is a double grace, and her continent mind cannot be valued. Forego not a wife and good woman, for her price is above gold. As the fun when it arifeth in the high heaven, fo is the beauty of a good wife. As the clear light is upon the holy candleftick, fo is the beauty of the face in ripe age. As the golden pillars are upon fockets of filver, fo are the fair feet with a conftant heart. A filent and loving woman is a gift of the Lord, and there is nothing fo much worth as a mind well inftructed. A good wife is a good portion, which fhall be given to them who fear the Lord; he that getteth her beginneth a poffeffion, a help like unto himfelf, and fhe is a pillar of reft. If there be kindnefs, meeknefs, and comfort in her tongue, then is not her hufband like moft other men.

OF A WICKED WIFE.

An evil wife is as a yoke fhaken to and fro; he that hath hold of her is as though he held a fcorpion. A fhamelefs woman fhall be counted as a clog, but fhe that is fhamefaced will fear the Lord. Give me any plague, but the plague of the heart, or any wickednefs, but the wickednefs of a woman. I had rather dwell with a lion and a dragon, than keep houfe with a wicked woman. A loud crying woman and a fcold fhall be fought out to drive away enemies. A drunken woman and a gadder abroad caufeth great anger, and fhe will not cover her own fhame. A difhoneft woman contemneth fhame, but an honeft woman will reverence her hufband. A woman that honoureth her hufband fhall be counted wife of all; but fhe that fhameth him by her pride fhall be called ungodly of all. A wicked wife abateth the courage, maketh a heavy countenance, and a wounded heart. A woman that will not comfort her hufband in diftrefs maketh weak hands and feeble knees. As the climbing of a fandy way to the aged, fo is a wife full of words to a quiet man. Her hufband fhall fit amongft his neighbours, and when he heareth her

fhall

shall sigh bitterly. The wickedness of a woman changeth her face and darkeneth her countenance like sackcloth. The whoredom of a woman may be known in her looks and eyelids. All wickedness is but little to the wickedness of a woman; let the portion of a sinner fall upon her; if she go not as thou wouldest have her, cut her off from thy flesh, and give her a bill of divorce, and let her go.

DUTY OF THE RICH TO THE POOR.

———

My fon, defraud not the poor of his living, and make not the needy to wait long. The bread of the needy is their life; he that defraudeth him thereof is a man of blood; he that taketh away his neighbour's living flayeth him; and he that defraudeth the labourer of his hire is a blood-fhedder. Make not an hungry foul forrowful, neither provoke a man in his diftrefs. Add not more trouble to a heart that is vexed, and defer not to give to him that is in need. Reject not the fupplication of the afflicted, neither turn away thy face from a poor man. Help the poor for the commandments fake, and turn him not away becaufe of his poverty. Turn not away thine eye from the needy, and give him none occafion to curfe thee, for if he curfe thee in the bitternefs of his heart, his prayer fhall be heard by him who made him. He will not accept any perfon againft a poor man, but will hear the prayer of the oppreffed; he will not defpife the fupplication of the fatherlefs, nor the widow, when fhe poureth out her complaint. Do not the tears run down the widow's cheeks? and is not her cry againft them that caufe

them

them to fall ? The prayer of the humble pierceth the clouds, and till it come nigh he will not be comforted, and will not depart till the Moft High ſhall behold to judge righteouſly and execute judgment, for the Lord will not be ſlack, neither will the Almighty be patient towards them, till he has ſmitten in funder the loins of the unmerciful, and repaid vengeance to the heathen; until he have taken away the multitude of the proud, and broken the ſceptre of the unrighteous. My ſon, blemiſh not thy goodneſs, neither uſe uncomfortable words when thou giveſt any thing. Let it not grieve thee to bow down thine ear to the poor, and give him a friendly anſwer with meekneſs; deliver him that ſuffereth wrong from the hand of the oppreſſor; be not faint-hearted when thou ſitteſt in judgment; be as a father to the fatherleſs, and inſtead of a huſband to their mother; ſo ſhalt thou be as the ſon of the Moſt High, and he ſhall love thee more than thy mother doth. Fail not to be with them that weep, and mourn with them that mourn; be not ſlow to viſit the ſick, for that ſhall make thee beloved, and ſtretch thine hand to the poor, that thy bleſſing may be perfected. Whatſoever thou takeſt in hand, remember the end, and thou ſhalt never do amiſs.

ON FRIENDSHIP.

═══

IF thou wouldſt get a friend, prove him firſt; and be not over haſty to credit him.

A faithful friend is a ſtrong defence, and he that hath found ſuch an one hath found a treaſure.

Nothing doth countervail a faithful friend, and his excellency is invaluable.

A faithful friend is the medicine of life, and they that fear the Lord ſhall find him.

Change not thy friend for any good, neither a faithful brother for the gold of Ophir.

Forſake not an old friend, for the new is not comparable to him. A new friend is as new wine; when it is old thou ſhalt drink it with pleaſure.

Do good unto thy friend before thou die, and according to thy ability ſtretch out thy hand, and give him.

Admoniſh thy friend, it may be he hath not ſaid it, and if he have, that he ſpeak it not again.

Admoniſh

Admonifh thy friend, for many times it is a flander, and believe not every tale.

Love thy friend, and be faithful unto him ; but if thou bewrayeft his fecrets, follow no more after him, for he is far off; he is as a roe efcaped out of the fnare.

Lend to thy neighbour in time of his need.

Keep thou thy word, and deal faithfully with him, and thou fhalt always find the thing neceffary for thee.

Forget not the friendfhip of thy furety, for he has given his life for thee.

Be faithful to thy neighbour in his poverty, that thou mayeft rejoice with him in his profperity; abide ftedfaft unto him in the time of his trouble. A mean eftate is not to be contemned, nor the rich that are foolifh to be had in admiration. I will not be afhamed to defend a friend, neither will I hide myfelf from him.

Ufe thy money for thy brother and thy friend, and let it not ruft under a ftone to be loft; defraud not thyfelf of a good day, and let not the part of a good defire pafs over thee.

AGAINST PRIDE, ANGER, AND STUBBORNNESS.

O Lord! Father and God of my life, give me not a proud look, but turn away from thy fervant always a haughty mind. The Lord hath caft down the throne of proud princes, and fet up the meek in their. ftead. The Lord hath plucked up the root of proud nations, and planted the lowly in their place. Pride was not made for man, nor furious anger for thofe that are born of a woman; pride is hateful before God and man, and by it doth one commit iniquity. Why is duft and afhes proud? He that toucheth pitch fhall be defiled therewith, and he that hath fellowfhip with a proud man fhall be like unto him.

In the punifhment of the proud there is no remedy, for the plant of wickednefs hath taken root in him. The beginning of pride is when one departeth from God, and his heart is turned away from his Maker; for pride is the beginning of fin, and he that hath it fhall pour out abomination. The ftrife of the proud ends in bloodfhedding, and their revilings are grievous to the ear. A furious man cannot be juftified, for the fway of his fury fhall be his deftruction. Strive not with an angry man, and go not with him into a folitary place, for blood is as nothing in his fight, and where there is no help, he will overthrow thee. Mockery and reproach are from the proud, but vengeance as a lion fhall lie in wait for them.

As the matter of fire is, fo it burneth, and as a man's ftrength is, fo is his wrath, and according to his riches his anger rifeth. A hafty contention kindleth a fire, and an hafty contention fheddeth blood. Strive not with a mighty man, left thou fall into his hands, nor with a man that is full of words, and heap not wood on his fire. Kindle not the coals of a finner, left thou be burnt with the flame of his fire. Rife not up in anger with an injurious perfon, left he lie in wait to entrap thee in thy words.

Jeft not with a rude man, left thy anceftors be difgraced. Rejoice not over thy greateft enemy being dead, but remember we die all. Bring not every man into thine houfe, for the deceitful man hath many trains; for he lieth in wait, and turneth good into evil, and in things worthy praife will he lay blame upon thee; of a fpark of fire a heap of coals is kindled, and a finful man layeth wait for blood. Take heed of a mifchievous man, for he worketh wickednefs, left he bring upon thee a perpetual blot.

Children being haughty through difdain and want of nurture do ftain the nobility of their kindred.

An

An obſtinate heart ſhall be laden with ſorrows, and the wicked man ſhall heap ſin upon ſin. He that revengeth ſhall find vengeance from the Lord, who will ſurely keep his ſins in remembrance. Forgive thy neighbour the hurt that he hath done thee, ſo ſhall thy ſins be forgiven; one man beareth hatred againſt another, and doth he ſeek pardon from the Lord? he ſheweth no mercy to a man who is like himſelf, and doth he aſk forgiveneſs of his own ſins? If he that is but fleſh nouriſh hatred, who will entreat for pardon for his ſins?

Remember thy end, and let enmity ceaſe; remember corruption and death, and abide in the commandments.

ON THE RIGHT OR WRONG USE OF THE TONGUE.

—

SWEET language will multiply friends, and a fair
speaking tongue will increase kind greetings. Re-
frain not to speak, when there is occasion to do
good, for by speech wisdom shall be known, and
learning by the words of the tongue. A wise man
shall promote himself to honour by his words, and
he that hath understanding shall please great men.
Be stedfast in thy mind, and let thy word be the
same; be swift to hear, and let thy life be sincere,
and with patience give answer. If thou hast understanding, answer thy neighbour, if not, lay thy
hand upon thy mouth; honour and shame are in
talk, and the tongue of man is his fall. He that
can rule his tongue shall live without strife, and he
that hateth babbling shall have less evil. Rehearse
not unto another that which is told unto thee, and
thou shalt fare never the worse. Whether it be to a
friend or a foe, talk not of other men's secrets, and if
even thou canst without offence, reveal them not.
If thou hast heard a word, let it die with thee, and
behold it will not burst thee. A fool travaileth
with a word; as a woman in labour of a child, so
will

will an unfeafonable tale be in the mouth of the unwife. The talking of a fool is like a burden in the way, but grace fhall be found in the lips of the wife. A tale out of feafon is as mufic in time of mourning; but correction by wifdom is never out of time.

As is a houfe deftroyed, fo is wifdom to a fool, and the knowledge of the unwife is as talk without fenfe. The inner parts of a fool are like a broken veffel, and he will hold no knowledge as long as he liveth. The knowledge of a wife man fhall abound like a flood, and his counfel is like a pure fountain of life. If a fkilful man hear a wife word, he will commend it, and add unto it, but as foon as one of no underftanding heareth it, it difpleafeth him, and he cafteth it behind his back. Doctrine unto fools is as fetters on the feet, and like manacles on the right hand. He that telleth a tale unto a fool fpeaketh to one in a flumber; when he hath told his tale, he will fay, what is the matter?

The lips of talkers will be telling fuch things as pertain not unto them, but the words of fuch as have underftanding are weighed in the balance. The hearts of fools are in their mouths, but the mouths of the wife are in their hearts. Learning unto a wife man is as an ornament of gold, and like a bracelet upon his right arm.

THE SCRIBBLER.

1ˢᵀ PAPER.

=====

Aɴᴏᴛʜᴇʀ Novel! Pray, have you read it, Sir? or
you? Who the deuce would? cried an elderly gentleman (laying down the news-paper, and taking
off his fpectacles) I have already, Sir, waded through
fuch an inundation of hobgoblin nonfenfe, of
haunted caftles, myfterious caverns, yawning
graves, bleeding ghofts, &c. that, had they not a
ready paffage out of my head, I fhould expect to
find my night-cap rife perpendicular from it, and
every hair turned white with horror; yes, yes, Sir,
fuch would be the effect every bloody-minded no-
vel-writer wifhes to inflict upon you; but I no
fooner fee the drift and cruelty of his intention,
than I grow enraged at my author, arm myfelf with
a coat of mail, not like Don Quixote, to fight my
opponents as giants, but prepared to difpute the
pafs with them, to ftrip off their *white fheets*, to
pluck out their *goggle eyes*, and fhew them as nature
defigned them. There are another fpecies of novel
writers, rejoined a pale-faced and emaciated lady,
far more difficult to combat, I mean your *profeffed*
fentimental authors, who moft ingenioufly rack
every

every corner of their brain to invent new tortures
for your nerves; who deliberately probe every fibre
in your heart, where, if any recent sorrow is lulled
or suppressed, it is again torn open. Against these
writers there is no appeal, for whilst there are readers
found who not only *chuse* to waste their time, but
like to be made unhappy into the bargain, there
will ever be plenty of authors ready to assist them
to the utmost of their wishes in the accomplish-
ment of both. At the conclusion of this ha-
rangue, I observed the gentleman who had uninten-
tionally brought on this volley of abuse (by simply
asking, have you read the new novel) slily slip two
volumes into the chaos of trash upon the counter,
and take two others from the shelf, saying, as he
hobbled out, there, Mr. Librarian, I have taken Joe
Miller's Jests and the Pilgrim's Progress, as I begin to think it is better after all to be merry and
wise than sad and silly. And a good exchange he
has made indeed, replied a lady; for the two books
he had before singled out, I perceive, were the
Sorrows of Werter, and the Self-Tormentor. As
I had gotten possession of an arm-chair by the fire-
side, to observe the important business of a circulating library, I found myself too comfortable, and
too well entertained, to quit my seat hastily, particularly as at that instant three beautiful young
ladies pressed in, and with animated and inquiring
countenances requested the catalogue to chuse
their studies from, when all crowding over it, the

talleft of the three called out, Oh, my deareft Lydia,
I have now met with the book I have been mad
after, and abfolutely dying for. I am told by Mrs.
Dozer (who reads every thing) it is a moft enchant-
ing novel, and fo affecting, it is enough to break
your heart. She affured me fhe was blind with
crying, and that poor Counfellor Winifred de-
clared it had deftroyed his appetite, and broke
his night's reft for fome time, for there are
feven volumes. Seven volumes! repeated my
elderly gentleman; feven plagues and feven fu-
ries! No fooner had this exclamation efcaped his
lips, than the three young ladies burft into a loud
laugh, and cried, " What a gig he is, I quizzed him
the inftant I came in."

A young lady in a loofe morning drefs now trip-
ped in, and whifpered a young man behind the
counter, but not fo low but I could hear her en-
quiry was for the *Monk*; and on the man affuring
her all his fets were from home, fhe cried, " that is
deplorable indeed ; to be kept juft at the moft cri-
tical and interefting part waiting for the laft volume; I wifh your mafter would buy more fets of
a novel on which fo much is faid and written." I
was forry to hear my friend in the corner had not
overheard the whifper of the fair enquirer, being
well affured he would not have fuffered a book of
fuch an alarming tendency (particularly in the hands
of fo young a ftudent) to have been named without his admonition to the reader, and his anathema
againft

againſt the writer. I felt pained (on contemplating the innocent countenance of the young lady) to think that blaſphemy and obſcenity ſhould ever meet her eye? I wiſhed to ſpeak and ſtop the contagion of the evil, as it ſeemed as yet not to have diffuſed its baneful influence; but to accoſt her, and to counſel her, would be uncommon, and be deemed impertinent. How ſuperior, thought I, are thoſe characters, who, regardleſs of the punctilios of breeding, will dare to do good to their fellow creatures, by obtruding their advice unaſked. With this reflection I aroſe diſſatisfied with myſelf, and having loſt all the comfort, quitted the amuſements, of my arm-chair. In my way home I tried to divert my mind by a walk through the park; it was in vain; the young lady and her companion the Monk occupied my mind too much to admit of it. I now accuſed myſelf of a breach of chriſtianity in not warning her of the dangerous tendency of ſuch ſtudies to young and unformed minds; I lamented the faſhions of the world, which lead us to comply with the follies and vices of it, inſtead of guarding ourſelves and others from them. In purſuing this thought, the following lines occurred, which I put down with a pencil:

Of all the fooliſh vain pretences, &c.

N. B.—See the verſes on *What the World will Say*, in the Collection of Poems.

Upon

Upon my return home (and after my evening's nap) the laughable complaints and injuries of the felf-tormented novel-readers, and the hardened cruelty and eafe, with which the authors of the calamities beftow them upon their votaries, appeared in fo truly ridiculous a light to my fancy, that finding it was determined into a fyftem of diftreffing and terrifying on one fide, and chufing to be diftreffed and terrified on the other, I bethought me that a written prefcription for the advantage of young beginners might not be unacceptable.

Would you a lucky Novel make, &c.

Note.—See the Receipt to write a Novel, amongft the Poems.

THE SCRIBBLER.

IIND PAPER.

I MUST confefs there are few things that more ex-
cite my wonder, or raife my fpleen, than feeing
(which I frequently do) a number of people met
together under the femblance of mirth and friendfhip, but in effect to diftrefs and terrify each other.
When children, through the carelefſnefs of their
parents, and the folly of their nurfes, tell each other
ftories of ghofts and hobgoblins, till they dare not
look behind them, I pity the children, and condemn the parents, &c.; but when I fee a fet of
what we call rational creatures, that is, people at
their full growth, in a high rank of life, and fup-
pofed to be in their right minds, met together in
affembly, after many hours fpent in adorning their
perfons, as if to make themfelves pleafing to each
other; I fay, when I hear them at the fame time they
are fitting down to cards, begin in the moft calm and
deliberate manner to relate accounts fhocking to hu-
manity, of horrid murders, dreadful accidents, total
ruin, deaths, and burials of their friends and inti-
mate acquaintance, with as much eafe as they
would

would read the weekly bills of mortality, I am at
firſt in doubt whether I am not in the infernal regions, or hearing the Witches in Macbeth croak
round their cauldron,

Double, double, toil and trouble, &c.

But alas, I am ſoon brought to my recollection
by ſome particular or familiar recital of diſtreſs,
which would entirely overpower me, did I not feel
myſelf rouſed with indignation for the violence
committed on the feelings of human nature, that
ſo far am I from meeting that relief or relaxation
from my own *heartfelt* griefs and cares, which I
came to ſeek for in ſociety, that I return home
enervated, harraſſed, and diſappointed, after being
ſucceſſively torn by every different paſſion which can
invade or make wretched the human breaſt ; would
but theſe criers of death and murders meet together in a ſelect ſociety, I would engage that no
one of them would come away leſs happy than
they went to it, on the contrary, each would have
had their particular gratification in relating the
different misfortunes of their friends and acquaintance ; for it is a certain fact, that theſe diſperſers of
calamities, or Pandora's of ſociety, never partake
in the diſtreſſes they relate ; but when it happens,
as it frequently muſt, in a mixt company, that
ſome of the neareſt connections to thoſe reported
to be ſlain, drowned, ruined, &c. are preſent, the
whole company is then thrown into the utmoſt
conſternation. I was the other night witneſs to a

ſcene,

fcene, at a party of this kind, which I fincerely pray
may never befal me again ; I was juft feated at a
whift table, with a moft amiable friend of mine,
when a lady of rank, who piques herfelf on having
the earlieft intelligence, chanced to be fet down
with us ; fhe was no fooner feated, than fhe began
in the moft confequential manner to inform us, fhe
had that inftant heard Ad——l S———'s fhip of
an hundred guns had taken fire, and every foul on
board had perifhed.   My poor friend, who was the
wife of this worthy Admiral, that inftant fell back
fenfelefs, and to all appearance dead.   The confufion
and furprize of the company you may eafily fuppofe.   I attended to little elfe but the victim of this
horrid tale, who, indeed, I feared in my diftraction
was too far gone to be recovered by any efforts
that a phyfician then prefent could ufe to reftore
her, but through the mercy of Providence fhe at
length opened her eyes; but the agonies of grief
with which fhe ftruggled, upon again coming to
her fenfes, are too painful to me to defcribe, were
it poffible.   She was immediately carried home,
when after being fome days confined to her bed in
a fever, in a ftate little fhort of frenzy, fhe was
fuddenly reftored to reafon and happinefs by a
letter from the Admiral himfelf, dated fince the
receipt of the information, acquainting her he was
perfectly well, and had not met with the leaft ac-
cident to their fleet fince the time of their embar-
kation.   Various other misfortunes of this kind
                                                            could

could I recite, at many of which I have been prefent ; but to a mind poffeffed of any feelings, the
one I have named is fufficient to fhew the juftice
of the complaint, and the unfeeling mind will (I
fear) never be brought to reafon.

THE SCRIBBLER.

IIIᵈ PAPER.

———

THOUGH there is no one quality with which the human mind is endowed, more amiable than fenfibility, yet I have often been led to doubt, whether the poffeffor of it is moft to be envied or pitied ; thus far is certain, that a perfon without fenfibility can never be an object of our affection or efteem ; but then being wrapt up in himfelf, he may with a heedlefs indifference enjoy more negative happinefs than one alive to all the finer feelings can poffibly do, by how much more the griefs and forrows of this prefent ftate weigh heavier in the balance than the joys and pleafures of it. Man was undoubtedly defigned by his Maker to partake in the griefs, as well as fhare in the joys of his fellow creatures; to rejoice with thofe who do rejoice, and weep with thofe who weep, is invariably the language of holy writ; but never are we promifed that the joys of this world fhall exceed the forrows of it, on the contrary, we are told, in various paffages like this, that man is born to trouble, as the fparks fly upwards, &c. &c.; but I mean not that reflections like thefe fhould deprefs our fpirits, but they fhould ferve to ftrengthen our refolutions and affections,

affections, and animate us to share with and affist our fellow creatures in bearing their burthens through this state of trial.

I was a few evenings ago led into a difcourfe on this fubject with a friend of mine, poffeffed of a refined underftanding and an elegant turn for poetry. I could well perceive he felt the fubject, and that he dwelt with great force and energy of expreffion on it ; but I well knew he had drank deep in the cup of adverfity, and that he owned a moft expanded and benevolent heart ; therefore finding our converfation called forth too much of thofe feelings, which, though they are the greateft ornaments of human nature, fhould not be fuffered to exhauft and prey upon her, I fuddenly changed the difcourfe, and begged my friend to ftep with me to the Coffee Houfe, where I many evenings pafs an hour in chatting and reading the papers; but my poor friend did not, however, fuffer the fubject to efcape his thoughts, for I was agreeably furprized next morning by finding the following copy of verfes on my breakfaft table, which I fend your readers, thinking them a far better definition of the effects of fenfibility than any thing further I can add on the fubject.

N. B.—For the verfes, fee the Ode to Senfibility, amongft the Poems.

F I N I S.